Intasimi Warriors Book One

MWIKALI AND THE FORBIDDEN MASK

SHIKO NGURU

First published in the United Kingdom in 2022 by Lantana Publishing Ltd., Oxford.
www.lantanapublishing.com | info@lantanapublishing.com

American edition published in 2022 by Lantana Publishing Ltd., UK.

Text © Shiko Nguru, 2022
Artwork & Design © Lantana Publishing, 2022

Cover and internal illustrations by Melissa McIndoe

The moral rights of the author and artist have been asserted.

Distributed in the United States and Canada by Lerner Publishing Group, Inc.
241 First Avenue North, Minneapolis, MN 55401 U.S.A.
For reading levels and more, look for this title at www.lernerbooks.com
Cataloging-in-Publication Data Available.

ISBN: 978-1-913747-93-0

Printed and bound in the Czech Republic.

 Lantana

For my father,
Prof. Godfrey Mbiti Nguru

(I hope this makes up for
not becoming a lawyer)

Intasimi Warriors Book One

MWIKALI AND THE FORBIDDEN MASK

SHIKO NGURU

The ~~Freak~~ Chameleon

You can hide a lot behind a smile. And as Mwikali stood in front of the mirror that morning, she practiced all the different types of smiles she could think of.

The first smile made her look overly excited and far too eager, like a puppy panting for a frisbee. The next was impossibly sweet and wide-eyed in a way that made her look half-crazy. And the last smile was so tight and forced that she might as well have been holding a neon sign above her head letting everyone know she was hiding something.

None of the smiles were believable. So, Mwikali dropped the corners of her mouth and took in a deep breath. *Plan B: no smile.* Instead, she would try not to be seen at all. Her new plan was to be the unsmiling, plain, ordinary girl who nobody noticed. She was going to fade into the background. Be invisible. Disappear. It was the only way to make sure nobody discovered the truth about her.

"Mwikali!" Her mom's voice rang out from outside her bedroom. "Hurry up or you'll miss the van!"

Mwikali scooped up the backpack resting at her feet. "I'll be right there!" she yelled, before turning back to the mirror.

Scanning her reflection, she smoothed down her school uniform for the umpteenth time. The girl in the mirror looked as normal as could be. She had the height of a normal twelve year old. Wore a normal uniform — white blouse, red tie, blue skirt with a matching sweater. And even though her almond-shaped eyes were larger than most, they were perfectly suited to her deep brown face.

Mwikali grabbed a hair band and tied her thick, jet-black Afro into a ponytail, making sure she rounded out and tucked in all the loose ends, forming a tight bun on top of her head. Her scalp ached in protest but Mwikali pushed through the discomfort. As much as she loved her loose, fluffy hair, it had to remain hidden away. The plan was to be as unnoticeable as possible.

She clenched and unclenched her hands, worry clouding her face. Everything about the girl in the mirror looked normal, but deep down she knew that she wasn't normal at all.

I'm a freak. A dangerous, very not-normal freak.

The memory of names others had called her brought a familiar tightness to Mwikali's chest. She crumpled handfuls of skirt in her clammy hands as her heart began to thump.

Stop this! she commanded herself. She couldn't lose it. Not today. She wanted today to go well. Needed it to go well. Today was her first day at a new school. It was a chance to start afresh. A chance to leave behind all the horrible things that had happened at her last school. For that to happen, she needed to act normal. Boring even. She had to hide who she really was.

"Haraka, haraka, Mwikali!" Mom called out, more urgently than before. "Hurry up or you'll be late!"

With one last glance at the mirror, Mwikali exhaled sharply and then swung her bedroom door open. "Coming!"

The sweet scent of freshly fried dough wafted out of the kitchen and into her nose as soon as she stepped outside.

"Mandazis!" she cheered, bounding down the stairs of the three-bedroom townhouse she lived in with her mom and auntie.

Mandazis were Mwikali's favorite pastries in the whole world. They were an extra special treat with a mouthwatering smell, powerful enough to push out her worries and put a real smile on her face. She loved mandazis even more than she loved donuts. And *that* was no small deal.

Mom claimed that mandazis and donuts were more or less the same thing, but Mwikali— a pastry fanatic— knew better. Mandazis were shaped like triangles, not circles, they didn't have gaping holes in the middle and they always had a little bit of spice added to their sweetness. They were both delicious, but totally different. At least to Mwikali.

First days of school didn't usually count as mandazi-type days, but then again, this wasn't an ordinary first day of school. Today was her first day at a new school, in their new *permanent* home town. For the first time ever, Mwikali would be joining a school and staying there.

Thanks to Mom's job at an airline company, they had never lived anywhere for longer than a couple of years. Mom had scored a big promotion a few months earlier and had been offered the opportunity to move back to the city that she was raised in, the city where Mwikali had been born — Nairobi, the capital city of Kenya. The airline had moved them into their new home and even gotten Mwikali a spot at Savanna Academy, one of the most prestigious schools in East Africa.

Now, after a life spent bouncing around from country to country — the United Kingdom, United States, United Arab Emirates, China — she was finally going to be able to settle in one place long enough to get used to it.

"Morning!" Auntie said brightly, once she reached the bottom of the stairs.

"Morning, Auntie!" Mwikali replied, her wide grin taking up most of the space on her face. "Mom's making mandazis!"

Auntie laughed and continued sweeping the carpet. "I knew that smell would bring you downstairs fasta, fasta."

Mwikali giggled as she skipped through the living room and through to the kitchen. Although Auntie had only been living with them for two months, she already knew Mwikali better than most.

Auntie wasn't her *real* auntie. That is, she wasn't related to Mwikali by blood. Auntie was what everyone called nannies in Kenya. And even though it had taken Mwikali some time to get used to the idea of having a full-time nanny, she had come to love having Auntie around. Unlike the babysitters she'd had in the past, Auntie treated her more like a friend than just some kid she'd been hired to look after.

"Morning, Mwikali!" Mom trilled.

The air inside the kitchen was hot, steamy and inviting. Mwikali licked her lips as she eyed the big bowl of mandazis already sitting on the counter. "Mom, I'm going to eat like ten of those," she warned.

Mom chuckled as she took the last batch out of the fryer. Kenyan pop music was playing from a Bluetooth speaker in the corner and Mom was wiggling her hips to the beats like she always did. She was listening to her favorite music group — Sauti Sol. She loved them almost as much as Mwikali loved mandazis.

It had been a long time since Mwikali had seen her mother looking so happy. Mom had always talked about having a "forever home" in her birth country someday. And now that she had completed her management training and they were finally there, she couldn't wait to introduce Mwikali to every single aspect of Kenyan life — loud Sauti Sol music included. Being home and knowing that Mwikali would grow up around Kenyan family and traditions made her happier than ever.

Since the move, Mwikali had already met a bunch of cousins she didn't even know existed. They had all been really friendly and had tried to make Mwikali feel like she belonged. But Mwikali had never really felt like she belonged anywhere. For as long as she could remember, she had always been different. She had always been the new kid. The outsider. And at her last school, she had even gotten a new title — the freak.

Things would be different here, though. She was

going to make sure of it. Her plan was already in place: avoid attention, blend into the background, disappear. Just like a chameleon.

"*Ayyyyeeeee*," Mom hollered, waving her hands around in the air. She was really going at it with the dancing, even doing that cringey dance move adults love to do where they pucker their lips and twirl their butts all the way down to the floor.

"Oh my gosh, Mom, *stopppp*," Mwikali moaned, slapping her hand over her eyes. She didn't need to see that. Nobody did.

Mom threw her head back and laughed before standing back up and serving her a plate of piping hot mandazis. "Happy first day of school!" she sang. "Sorry I have to leave for this work trip. I can't believe I'll miss your first few days!"

"Ohhh, you're feeling guilty about abandoning me on my first week of school. *That's* why you're making mandazis!" Mwikali said, with a cheeky smile.

"No, that isn't true, although I *am* sorry about that," Mom said, poking her daughter's nose. "It's because today marks a new beginning for you. You'll be a lot happier here. I just know it!"

A new beginning for you? You'll be a lot happier here? Mwikali's stomach did a flip. She knew exactly what her mom meant and immediately realized what all this was about. The mandazis, the sing-songy voice, the fact that Mom was being so *extra* — all of it. It wasn't just about the first day of school or settling down in Kenya or the fact that she was leaving for a three-day trip. *This?* This was about what happened to her last year.

Mwikali felt her hands start to get sweaty again. The last thing she wanted was to get into this conversation with her mom. But it was too late.

"Mwikali, I know that last year was hard for you," Mom began, her eyes creased with concern. "Amanda was your best friend and I know that when she had her medical emergency, things got really tough for you at school. Although, I'm still not sure I know why..."

Mom's voice trailed off as she studied Mwikali's face, searching for answers like she always did. Answers that never came.

How could Mwikali tell her mom that she was the reason Amanda had had a medical emergency in the first place? That, without knowing it, she had almost killed her best friend? How could she explain to her that there was something freakish and evil inside her — something she didn't fully understand — that hurt people?

She couldn't. The best thing she could do was bury that part of her and try not to talk or even think about it again. Maybe then it would disappear.

Mwikali stuffed her face full of mandazis to avoid having to give her mom the answers she was looking for. Then, holding a napkin over her mouth, she started to back out of the kitchen. "I'm really late. Don't wanna miss the van," she said, in a muffled voice.

"Ai! But you've hardly eaten," Mom complained. "And you haven't even had a cup of tea!"

Mwikali was already outside the kitchen door. "See you when you get back from your trip! Love you!"

Without waiting for a response, Mwikali whirled around on her heels and sprinted to the door. She managed to squeeze in a "Bye, Auntie!" before slamming it shut behind her.

Her escape didn't feel complete until she had jogged down the driveway and exited their compound entirely. Only then, while leaning against the cool metal gate on the outside of their property, did she breathe out a sigh of relief.

She walked to the curb, thinking that Mom was definitely right about one thing. Today marked a new beginning for her. Amanda, everything that happened at her old school...all of that was in the past. And she was going to do everything she could to keep it there.

A steady line of school vans soon began to roll past

her. They all looked the same: mustard yellow on the outside with twelve seats on the inside. The only difference between them was the school logos painted on their sides. Mwikali shifted impatiently from foot to foot as she kept an eye out for the Savanna Academy van.

And she wasn't alone. Other kids from the twenty or so houses that made up their neighborhood estate were waiting outside for their vans, too. Although she recognized most of them, they had no idea who she was. She had only ever seen them from her bedroom window where she would watch them as they played in the street. She had yet to work up the courage to introduce herself.

Though she looked like a Kenyan and had a Kenyan name, Mwikali was painfully aware that she didn't talk or act like one. She didn't talk or act like she was from anywhere in particular, really. Even her accent was a mishmash of all the different countries she had lived in.

Mom insisted that she would have an easy time making friends at Savanna Academy because of its "richly diverse population of international students." She probably just hoped that Mwikali's not-quite-Kenyan-ness wouldn't stand out as much among a bunch of actual not-Kenyans.

A slight drizzle started to fall, making Mwikali wonder if she had made a mistake by leaving the house so early. Just as she turned around to go back inside, she heard the sound of slippers clapping toward her.

"Mwikali, wait! I have something for you!" Mom wheezed as she ran down the driveway and threw open the front gate.

Her hand was stretched out toward Mwikali, holding something that looked vaguely familiar. By the time Mwikali had made sense of what it was, her mom had already thrust it into her hands.

It was a weapon. *The* weapon.

The one Mwikali had nearly killed her best friend with.

The ~~Weapon~~ Sketchbook

Mwikali struggled to remember if the leather-bound book resting on her palms had always felt so heavy. It felt like she was carrying a tombstone.

Her fingers trembled as she stared at the sketchbook's front cover where her name was printed in shimmery block letters. What she felt in that moment was the complete opposite of the excitement that had exploded in her when Mom had first presented her with the book.

It was the morning of her 11th birthday and she had screamed when she had found the sketchbook at the bottom of a gift bag stuffed with tissue wrap. They had been living in Chicago at the time and Mom had ordered the custom-made book for her from some fancy stationery store. It was the perfect sketchbook for a budding artist. And it had her name written on it, too! It was the best birthday gift ever. Or so she thought.

Back then, she didn't know that it was far more than just a book. She hadn't yet discovered that, in her hands, the sketchbook was a powerful and deadly weapon.

"I found it in the trash," Mom was saying, her brows

knitted tightly together. "I don't know why you would throw it away, Mwikali. You're such a great artist! So, I took it out and saved it for your first day of school — for good luck."

Mwikali could hardly hear anything her mom was saying over the whooshing sound filling her ears. All the painful memories from the past year were flooding back into her mind. She remembered how much she had adored that sketchbook. How it had felt like an extension of her, and how she would often get lost in it for hours, sketching all of her problems and worries away.

The sketchbook had become the one constant in her ever-changing world. It had been *her* forever home.

Sadness shuddered through Mwikali as she remembered the horrible day when everything had changed. The day that she and her best friend, Amanda, had gotten into an argument.

"Something is off with you," Mwikali had said to her friend. "I don't know what it is...but something about you is weird."

That one word — "weird" — is what started the argument.

"Look who's talking?" Amanda had barked, her eyes full of anger. "Everyone knows you're the weirdo."

Mwikali tried to explain that she wasn't saying that

Amanda was weird, only that something was weird about her that day. But it was no use. Amanda had stormed off, leaving Mwikali to spend the rest of the lunch break alone, drawing.

After lunch, some kids in class had pointed out that the girl in her sketchbook looked like Amanda. When they asked Mwikali why she had drawn her best friend lying in a hospital bed when she wasn't even sick, she had brushed them off. She hadn't meant to draw anyone in particular, let alone Amanda. In fact, she hadn't even realized what or who she was drawing until she was done!

But then, something terrible had happened. Amanda's appendix had burst, right in the middle of class. She had been rushed to hospital, just like in Mwikali's drawing.

Rumors had started to spread even before the ambulance arrived. By the end of the day, the whole class had heard how Mwikali had cursed her best friend, causing her appendix to rupture. And by the end of the week, everyone in school had started calling Mwikali a freak. Even Amanda, who made a full recovery, went on to tell anyone who would listen that Mwikali had tried to kill her through a drawing.

At first, Mwikali had thought it was all just a horrible coincidence. It had to be. But then it had happened again: she had drawn a picture of the street outside their apartment building blanketed with snow. That evening, she had watched in horror as an emergency news broadcast warned of a blizzard raging across the Midwest and headed their way. It had hit Chicago the following morning.

In the end, Mwikali had had no choice but to believe what all the kids were saying about her. She was a freak. And the sketchbook? It was her weapon.

There was only one thing she could do to make sure nothing like that ever happened again. One morning before school, she had gone around to the back of their Chicago apartment building and tossed the sketchbook into a large dumpster. And to make doubly sure that she couldn't hurt anyone ever again, Mwikali had vowed never to pick up a drawing pencil for as long as she lived.

She thought she had taken care of it and that that part of her life was well and truly behind her. But now…

Her mother's shrill voice brought Mwikali crashing back to the present. "Mwikali, get in!" She was pointing at the Savanna Academy van that had stopped in front of them. "Bye! Love you! See you on Friday when I'm back!"

Mwikali tried to respond but her throat was too tight. All she could manage was a slight wave goodbye as her mom walked away.

The van driver tapped the steering wheel impatiently as she squeezed into the back row of the mostly empty van and flopped down into a seat by the window. Her mind spun as she clutched the sketchbook to her chest. She thought she'd gotten rid of it! For good! And now here she was, about to take it into her brand new school — her brand new life!

Mwikali fought a rising panic as the van made its way through other estates, picking up more kids. She couldn't shake the feeling that something bad was about to happen.

"You're in my seat, new girl."

She jerked her head up at the rough voice. A skinny boy with a narrow face stood hunched over in the next row of seats, glaring at her.

"Are you deaf? I said, you're in my seat, *noob*," he repeated angrily. Noticing her puzzled eyebrows, he rolled his eyes and added, "Noob means newbie. That's what you are, right? A new girl?"

Mwikali folded her hands. She knew what a noob was. Almost every Gen Z kid did. It wasn't the first time she'd been called one, either. She was just confused as to why this boy thought he had a right to her seat.

"There are no assigned seats on school vans," she said firmly, surprising herself with the sudden flare of courage. She didn't know all the rules at Savanna Academy, but she was a hundred percent sure that she was right on this one. Well, more like sixty percent.

The boy's eyebrows shot up and his mouth popped open slightly. He was obviously not used to being stood up to. His chest heaved for a few seconds before he spoke again.

"Do you know who I am?" he asked, tapping his forefinger against the plastic badge on his chest. It was green, shaped like a knight's shield, and had the word "Prefect" written on it.

Mwikali had no idea what a prefect was, but she was determined not to let this dude bully her out of her seat. "Whoever you are, I'm sure it doesn't give you the right to be mean to people."

A honk from the van driver startled them both. He motioned for the boy to sit down and strap in.

With his eyes burning with anger and his mouth pressed into a straight line, the narrow-faced boy started to turn away from her and then stopped. "I'm Charo," he said, through gritted teeth. "Remember that name. Because you'll regret this."

He turned around and slumped into the next available window seat, leaving Mwikali squirming with unease. Could anything else go wrong? School hadn't even started yet and she had already acquired both a weapon of magical destruction *and* a mortal enemy.

By the time they arrived at Savanna Academy, Mwikali was convinced that the day was not going to go at all the way she had hoped it would. She even considered throwing the sketchbook away. It would have been easy enough to do. All she needed was to stretch out her hand and drop the book into one of the many bins sprinkled around the school. Just dump it and keep walking. Never look back. There were so many students crisscrossing the large school quad on their way to class that nobody would even notice if she did.

But Mwikali couldn't bring herself to do it. Even after everything that had happened, the sketchbook — which she held pressed against her chest — still meant a lot to her. Having it back after so long made her realize just how lonely she had been without it. She couldn't bring herself to let go of it a second time.

"Good morning, Mwikali!" shouted the Headmaster, as he shuffled towards her from across the quad.

Mwikali did her best to brighten up her face, forced smile and all. "Good morning, Babu!"

Babu was what the headmaster of Savanna Academy preferred to be called. And with his white hair, wrinkly smile, thick glasses and old fashioned walking stick, the title of "Babu," which was Swahili for "grandfather," did in fact suit him more than that of headmaster.

"Welcome to Savanna Academy," Babu said, warmly. Then he scrunched his face and pointed at the name tag on Mwikali's sweater. All new students were asked to wear name tags for the first week of school and she had mindlessly written her name and stuck hers onto her sweater after the run in with Charo.

"What's this?" Babu asked, frowning. "Who's...Kali?"

Mwikali had been so distracted that she had put down the name that the teachers at some of her other schools insisted she go by. "Oh," she muttered, self-consciously. "I'm used to going by Kali because it's easier for people to pronounce."

"Mwikali is a beautiful name," Babu said, shaking his head. Then, while jiggling his cane at her, added, "Never water yourself down to make other people more comfortable. Stay whole, stay true, and let them adjust to you. Hmm?"

They both smiled as she nodded and ripped the name tag off. It wasn't often that she was made to feel like it was okay to just be herself, and yet Babu had done it so easily. She could see why everyone at Savanna Academy loved him so much. "Thanks, Babu."

"Anytime. Come to my office on Friday and tell me all

about your first week, eh? I hope you have a good one. Now, hurry to class," he said, waving his hand. "Kwaheri, Mwikali."

"Bye, Babu. See you around."

Mwikali continued to thread her way through the quad, eventually spotting the door of her Grade Six classroom. Each grade was split into five streams to keep the individual classes small. Each stream was named after one of the Big Five animals: leopard, lion, buffalo, rhino and elephant. Mwikali was in Chui, the leopard class.

Dread twisted her gut as she reached the classroom door. No matter how many times she switched schools, this part — the one where she had to walk into a new classroom for the first time — never got any easier. The swarm of butterflies in her stomach soon began their lively dance.

Mwikali teetered on the threshold for a few seconds, listening to the loud chatter coming from inside the room and gulping down a series of shaky breaths. She just needed to get through this part and then everything else would be easier. At least that's what she hoped.

With one deep, calming breath, and as much resolve as she could muster, Mwikali stuck her chin out and walked into her new class.

A loud snicker caught her attention only a few steps in. "You're in my class, noob?" said Charo, with a smirk. "I told you you'd regret it."

Mwikali felt her blood run cold. What were the odds that her new enemy would be in her class? This day just kept going from bad to epically worse.

She was determined not to let Charo see her sweat. Bullies were like wolves — they could smell fear. She had to fake it. Pretending not to be bothered by him in the least, she rolled her eyes and looked past him. It worked! With a click of his tongue, he turned and looked away.

Mwikali quickly scanned the room full of evenly spaced desks. They were the kind of heavy, wooden school desks that had a lid at the top with a drawer space for storing books inside. A wave of relief washed over her when she spotted an empty one at the back of class.

Perfect, Mwikali thought. Operation blend-in-and-disappear is a go.

As she weaved her way toward the free desk, she noticed a trio of kids staring at her. A couple of them even exchanged looks and whispers when she passed by.

Her stomach cramped. What now? And why was the empty desk right next to them?

Mwikali did her best to act calm as she slid into her seat. She could feel the three sets of curious eyes following her, watching her every move as she sank down behind the desk.

One of them cleared his throat. Loudly. He was trying to get her attention. Mwikali forced herself to meet his gaze and found his lips curved into a knowing smile. The smile of someone who knew a secret. *Her* secret?

Fear surged through Mwikali, driving her up and out of her seat. She searched the room with darting eyes, desperately hoping for somewhere else to sit.

The boy who had cleared his throat suddenly stood up, a crooked smile etched on his face. Mwikali's heart leaped into her throat. Memories of being bullied at her last school flashed through her mind. This was how it always started, with one kid making the first approach — the first dig — and then inviting everyone else to pile on. She couldn't let that happen. Couldn't let him get close enough to try.

Right as he started walking toward her, Mwikali saw it. A free desk on her far left. She wasted no time and sprinted for it, bumping up against chairs and annoyed students as she barreled across the room.

She collapsed into her new seat just as Babu walked into the classroom.

"Good morning!" he said, with a cheerful wave of his walking stick. "I'm still looking for a class teacher for you. Until I find one, you'll have me. Now, let's all sit down so we can get started."

As Babu settled into the teacher's desk, Mwikali stole a glance to her right. She watched as the boy paused for a moment and then slowly walked back to his seat. He shook his head as if amused, and whispered something to his friends. They all laughed, eyes fixed steadily on her.

Dread knotted Mwikali's insides, making her body feel as tight as a drum.

Something had almost happened.

Somehow, those kids knew about her past, maybe even about her secret. She sensed it, right down to her bones. Just like she sensed that her little escape wouldn't be enough to stop them.

This wouldn't be the end of it.

In fact, she feared that it was only the beginning.

The ~~Teacher~~ Monster

For the next few days, Mwikali did everything she could to avoid those three. She spent her morning and lunch breaks locked away in the girls' washroom and was the first inside the school van at home time. Anything to stay clear of them.

By the time Friday rolled around, Mwikali was feeling pretty good about Operation Chameleon. Her plan to be invisible had worked so well that even after a week of school, barely anyone besides Babu knew her name.

She felt relaxed when she walked into class on Friday morning and slid into her seat. Nobody had switched desks after the first day of school and Mwikali was more than happy to keep hers, which was far away from both the squad of staring kids and Charo, who made a point of reminding her every now and then that they were still enemies.

She had just unpacked her books, when one of the members of the squad — a girl who always tied her braids in twin space buns — lobbed a ball of paper onto her desk. When Mwikali looked up for an explanation, all she got was an impatient look from the girl, who pointed at the paper and then mouthed the words "Read it!"

Mwikali slowly un-crumpled the note and felt her blood turn to ice as she read what it said.

WE KNOW WHAT YOU ARE

She felt sick to her stomach.

How? HOW? Mwikali asked herself the same question over and over again. Even though she already suspected that they knew something about her past, she still couldn't understand *how* they did. Her last school was literally oceans away. How could they know what she had done?

Mwikali's eyes remained glued to the note as confusion circled inside her. Then, with shaky hands, she crumpled the note back up, opened her desk, and threw it inside. Operation Chameleon was officially over. Her secret was out.

She kept the lid of her desk open, not wanting to close it and have to face the girl and the rest of her squad. With her head bowed, she arranged and rearranged the contents of the drawer, until she caught sight of her sketchbook. It was at the very bottom of her desk, where she had hidden it on the first day of school. She had been determined not to touch it. But now... Now she wasn't so sure.

It was situations like these that had gotten Mwikali so attached to her sketchbook in the first place. Whenever she felt anxious or upset, drawing made her feel better. Safer. As if someone was giving her a warm hug. It was the exact feeling she needed at that very moment.

Mwikali pulled out her sketchbook and closed her desk, ignoring space bun girl's expectant stare. She ignored everything that was happening around her as she placed it gently on top of her desk. Biting on her lip, and wringing her jittery hands, she thought about how badly she missed the calm feeling that drawing gave her. Surely it wouldn't hurt to sketch a little bit before class?

She stole a quick glance at the wall clock: it was only 8:00 AM. Half an hour before their first lesson. And that's all she'd allow herself. Half an hour of drawing, just to calm her nerves.

Mwikali flipped her sketchbook open and felt a rush of excitement roll through her. The classroom, space bun girl, and everything else around her faded into the distance. All that mattered was her and her sketchbook. *Just half an hour*, she promised herself, as she picked up a drawing pencil and touched its dark tip to a blank page.

"Good morning!" Babu suddenly boomed.

"Me-eh!" Mwikali yelped in surprise, nearly falling out of her seat.

The class erupted into laughter. Charo, who was the loudest of them all, muttered "Silly noob" under his breath.

Mwikali shrank into her seat, wishing the floor would open up and swallow her. She hadn't heard Babu walk in. And why was he in class half an hour early anyway?

She checked the wall clock just to be sure: 8:31 AM. *What?* How? She looked down at her sketchbook. The page was no longer blank. A completed drawing stared back at her. That's how. She'd zoned out for a full thirty minutes while drawing. To her, it had felt like no time had passed at all.

Oh no. That was a bad sign. This wasn't supposed to happen. Not again. Not this year. Mwikali snapped her sketchbook shut and tossed it back inside her desk, vowing once again never to touch it.

Babu gave her a sympathetic smile before turning to the rest of the class. "Allow me to introduce your new class teacher, Mrs. Amdany." He gestured towards a tall woman standing beside him. "Mrs. Amdany, we are happy to finally have you here. The class is yours."

"Thank you," Mrs Amdany said, stiffly.

As Babu made his slow exit, Mwikali took a moment to study the new teacher. She had a hard face with sunken eyes and a mouth permanently curled down in a frown. Her attitude was decidedly sour and yet somehow familiar. Mwikali couldn't help but feel that she'd seen the woman somewhere before. But where exactly, she wasn't sure.

For a while, the room was dead silent. Only the steady, rhythmic sound of Babu's cane could be heard tapping along the floor as he left.

Mwikali continued to observe Mrs. Amdany. Her clothes — pleated gray pants and a feathery, black sweater — also looked familiar. If only she could remember where she had seen that exact same outfit before…

"As you have heard, I'm Mrs. Amdany," the woman started, when the door finally closed behind Babu. "And I don't tolerate foolishness."

Grabbing a piece of chalk from the teacher's desk, she turned to the blackboard and began to write. The chalk squeaked and screeched as she scraped the words "SWAHILI QUIZ" in large letters onto the board. A chorus of moans swept through the room.

Mwikali's mouth went dry. A quiz on the first week of school was bad enough, but a Swahili quiz when she could barely string ten words of the language together? This was her worst nightmare.

"QUIET!" Mrs. Amdany shrieked, spinning around to face the class.

That's when Mwikali realized where she'd seen the woman before. *Oh no.* No, no, no. This couldn't be happening. Her thoughts raced as she slid her hand into her desk and pulled out her sketchbook.

The hairs on the back of her neck stood up as she turned its pages, finally stopping on her latest drawing. Her eyes widened with recognition when she saw what — or rather *who* — she had drawn in her sketchbook several minutes before.

It was Mrs. Amdany. Mwikali had completed a full drawing of the woman before she had even seen her.

And that wasn't all. In Mwikali's drawing, Mrs. Amdany looked exactly like she did in real life — same pants, same sweater, and same stance in front of a blackboard with "SWAHILI QUIZ" written on it. There was just one detail that was frighteningly different.

In her sketchbook, Mrs. Amdany was a monster.

In the picture, the teacher's face was gray and crinkled. Her eyes — dark and hollow, like two bottomless pits. She had neither a nose nor a mouth. Instead, right underneath her haunting eyes, was a black, knife-like beak.

Mwikali gripped the sides of her desk as her breath shortened into shallow bursts. Eyes squeezed shut, she prayed desperately that what had happened the last time she drew in her sketchbook wouldn't happen again. Prayed that she didn't have the power to make horrifying things happen just by drawing them.

"You're not a freak. You're not a freak," she whimpered, before slowly opening her eyes and drawing them toward the front of the class. She needed to look at Mrs. Amdany. Needed to see if she had actually turned her teacher into a monster.

Starting from the classroom floor, she followed Mrs. Amdany's figure upwards. From her patent leather heels, up her gray pants to her plumy sweater, and then up her scrawny neck, stopping just before she got to her head.

Finally, after as much delay as possible, Mwikali's eyes flicked up to Mrs. Amdany's face. A sharp gasp escaped her lips. The empty eye sockets, the beak — they were all there. Right there, in front of her, stood the most nightmarish thing Mwikali had ever seen.

Mrs. Amdany was every bit the monster in real life that she was in the sketchbook.

Out of nowhere, Mrs. Amdany whipped around to face Mwikali. She cocked her head, seeming both curious and surprised, as if she couldn't understand how Mwikali could see — really *see* — her.

For a few terrifying seconds, Mwikali sat frozen in place and stared back. She could tell from the unconcerned background noise around her that none of the other kids could see what she was seeing. They were still grumbling about the quiz, completely oblivious to the fact that their teacher was now a hideous monster.

Mrs. Amdany's face turned even more menacing. She seemed angry that Mwikali was still looking at her — *seeing* her.

The woman's chest started to swell. Suddenly, she dropped her piece of chalk. Then, she lurched forward toward Mwikali with an angry shriek.

Before Mwikali knew what she was doing, she was on her feet. All she could think of was protecting herself and the other kids in the class from this...this *monster*.

She did the only thing she could think of. She stared right into Mrs. Amdany's beast-like face and lunged forward, letting out a wild scream of her own.

The instant she did, time stood still. A stunned silence filled the air. Mwikali was half standing, half crouching in the middle of the classroom, with every eye turned toward her.

She blinked, and when she opened her eyes, Mrs.

Amdany was human again. The monster was gone and only an angry-looking woman remained.

"Get out of my classroom!" Mrs. Amdany yelled, pointing at the door.

"I'm sorry," Mwikali spluttered. "I... I thought I saw— "

"GET OUT!" Mrs. Amdany exploded.

Tears sprung into Mwikali's eyes as she gathered her things. Jeers and snickers followed her as she stumbled out of the classroom and into the hallway.

Not only was she embarrassed beyond belief, but her heart ached at the thought that all her hopes of a fresh start had just been obliterated. There was no way she was ever going to live down that display of weirdness.

As she ran blindly to the washroom, Mwikali imagined space bun girl and her friends already spreading the intel they had on her to the rest of the class. Everybody would know what she was.

It may have been a new school but she was still the same freak. Nothing would ever change that.

Mwikali splashed water over her tear-streaked face. The coolness of it calmed her somewhat and she started to think logically through all that had just happened. Had Mrs. Amdany really turned into a monster?

Wondering if perhaps her hair bun was to blame for

squeezing hallucinations into her brain, Mwikali yanked
her hair tie off and shook out her big Afro. Some of the
tension in her head immediately eased away.

Yup, she thought as she smiled weakly at her
reflection, it must have been the hair. She might have
been a freak but even *she* couldn't make people turn into
monsters. It must have been some sort of illusion.

Mwikali felt a tiny ray of hope as she walked out of
the washroom. She would go to Babu's office for their
scheduled chat and explain away her outburst as a case
of new girl nerves — say that she was still super nervous
about her first week in a new school, and that it wouldn't
happen again. Babu would talk to Mrs. Amdany and
straighten everything out.

As for the other kids? Well, hopefully they'd get over
it and eventually just leave her alone. Maybe the bullying
wouldn't be too bad this time.

She was a few feet from Babu's office when she heard
a quick tapping sound. Without warning, someone
grabbed her from behind and shoved her through an
opening at her side. A door clicked shut at her back,
leaving her completely disoriented in a musty, dark
room.

As her eyes gradually adjusted to the lack of light,
Mwikali began to make out a bunch of items strewn all

over the floor: sweaters, lunch boxes, hockey sticks. She must be inside the school's Lost and Found room.

"Look at me."

A sharp voice came from the darkness, somewhere just ahead of Mwikali. A voice that curdled her blood and chilled her bones. A voice she knew. Mrs. Amdany's voice.

"Look. At. Me." the woman repeated.

Mwikali strained her eyes forward, bracing herself to see a monster, but Mrs. Amdany looked...normal.

"What are you?" the woman asked, sizing Mwikali up and down with disgust.

Mwikali shook her head. "I... I don't know what you mean."

"WHAT ARE YOU?" Mrs. Amdany screamed.

That's when it happened. Her eyes started to sink back into her head, descending deeper and deeper until only holes were left. Then, her nose and mouth fused together. They merged, then bulged, and finally hardened into a pointy beak.

Mwikali staggered backward, not stopping until her back was up against the door. Panic squeezed her chest as she fumbled around behind her for the door handle.

Mrs. Amdany made a clucking sound as she came closer, and when she was only a few inches away, leaned into Mwikali's face, filling the space between them with hot, stinking breath. "Something is coming," she hissed, her shriveled cheeks twitching with excitement. "Something not even *you* can stop!"

Just as she pulled open her black beak ready to snap at Mwikali's nose, the door swung open.

Mwikali, whose back had been pushed against the door in an attempt to get away from the beak, fell flat on the floor. Mrs. Amdany, also taken by surprise, quickly brought her arms up to shield her face from the sudden burst of light. When her hands lowered an instant later, she was human again.

Without another word — without even checking to see who had opened the door — she hopped over Mwikali and took off running down the hallway.

"You're welcome."

Mwikali looked up to see space bun girl and the two boys she was always with standing over her.

"*Hello?*" the girl said, crossing her arms. "I said, you're welcome? For saving your butt?"

"Thanks," Mwikali murmured, picking up her sketchbook and hugging it to her chest.

"Are you okay?" one of the boys asked. He was tall and looked way stronger than other sixth graders. "Did she hurt you?" he asked, sticking out his hand to help her up.

Mwikali shook her head and pushed to her feet, using his hand for support. The boy continued to search her face. "You sure you're good?" he asked, again.

"Yeah, I'm okay," she answered nervously, wondering if this fake concern was all a trick to gain her trust before the bullying started.

The other boy put a fisted hand over his mouth and cleared his throat — a sound she recognized immediately from that first day of class. The clearing-throat boy was short with a mop of curly brownish hair and a big cheeky grin. He was the complete opposite of the boy who had helped her up who was big and tall, wore his hair in a low cut fade, and had a quiet, serious look about him. One boy wore shorts that exposed his knobbly knees, while the other wore pants that made him look even more brawny.

With a lopsided smile still on his face, the short boy pointed at space bun girl. "That's Soni. She's fearless, bossy and has major trust issues." He turned to the big dude. "Baby Hulk over here is called Odwar. He's insanely strong, loyal and Mr. Popular here at Savanna Academy."

His smile grew even wider when he pointed at himself. "And I'm Xirsi. Lovable genius and the brains of this outfit."

"More like the mouth," Soni scoffed.

Xirsi stuck his tongue out at her before continuing. "Like we said in the note, we know what you are, Mwikali." He dropped his voice, and his smile. Grew gravely serious. "You need to come with us right now, before you get seriously hurt… Or worse."

The ~~Cursed~~ Seer

"We'll tell you everything you need to know after you tell us what was going on with you in class today," Soni announced, as soon as they had all sat down.

Not wanting to speak in the middle of the corridor, the four had walked out to the far edge of the sports field where they now huddled in a tight circle. With Mrs. Amdany having dismissed the class abruptly after Mwikali's outburst, they were free to do as they wished. The teacher hadn't even bothered to give an explanation for ending class early. She had just announced that class was over, packed up her things, and left. And while the other students had wandered out to sit on the benches by the cafeteria, the four of them had snuck out to the back of school where the field was.

Right across from the field's edge stood a thick mass of trees. Babu had pointed them out to Mwikali during her first school tour. He had told her that the thousand year old woods — called the Mugumo Tree Groves — were considered sacred by the local community.

Mwikali's nerves had tingled strangely when she had

looked out toward the groves during her tour. The same thing was happening now. The trees seemed to stare back at her, like they were somehow aware of her presence.

Xirsi elbowed her and tipped his head toward the groves. "People say they're haunted," he whispered. "They say that the spirits of the ancestors hover around the trees. If you enter the groves and the spirits decide you're not worthy?" He dragged his forefinger across his neck. "You're toast."

"Why do we have to meet here?" Mwikali asked, eyeing the nearby groves fearfully.

"Because what we're about to tell you is top secret and this is the most private place we could think of," Soni shot back, irritated. "Now, go ahead and tell us what your deal is."

Mwikali studied the three of them. They had just rescued her from Mrs. Amdany and showed no signs of wanting to bully her. In fact, they seemed curious, friendly even. She couldn't think of a reason to lie to them and found that she had no desire to, either. So, she took in a breath and then exhaled the words out.

"I make horrible things happen just by drawing them."

The words rushed out of her like air out of a pricked balloon. It was as if a year's worth of pressure had been building up inside her. And now, she was letting it all out. It felt good, so she rattled on.

"Every time I draw in my sketchbook, whatever I draw happens. Last year, I made my friend sick and caused a snowstorm. And then, this morning, I drew Mrs. Amdany as a bird-faced monster before I even met her. And then, she came to class and actually *turned* into a monster. But then, when I screamed, she turned back into a human and kicked me out of class. And I thought I was going crazy but then she chased me into the Lost and Found closet. That's when she changed back into monster mode and I think she wanted to hurt me? But then, you guys rescued me and were all like 'Come with us' and now here we are."

They stared at Mwikali in wide-eyed amazement as she went on to describe exactly what Mrs. Amdany had looked like. Their eyes expanded even more when she held open her sketchbook and showed them her drawing.

For a while, everything went quiet. Mwikali began to think the worst. That they had gone from simply being curious about her, to thinking that she was a complete nut job. Maybe now the bullying would start.

She began to close her sketchbook, ready to get out of there. "Sorry, this was a mistake. I'm not even sure what I saw. I'm probably just super nervous about being in a new schoo—"

Xirsi grabbed her sketchbook before she could finish and held it up to his crinkled nose. "Mrs. Amdany looked like *this*? That's insane!"

"I knew Mrs. Amdany was bad news from the moment I saw her," Soni said, shaking her head. "But even *I'm* shook right now. She's a *monster* monster."

Odwar pulled the sketchbook away from Xirsi and nodded approvingly. "You're a really good artist. This is the best drawing of a monster in true form I've ever seen. And I can't believe you can actually see them!"

Mwikali's eyes shifted from side to side. She couldn't believe what she was hearing. "You guys believe me? You're not...scared?"

Xirsi let out a high pitched laugh while Odwar simply grinned. "Scared? Why? I mean, we could already sense that she was evil. It's just crazy to see her true form like this."

"Yeah, and if I'm not wrong, I think Mwikali might be the only Intasimi who can actually see monsters in true form," Odwar said, excitedly.

"The only what?" Mwikali grabbed both sides of her head. She was having trouble keeping up with everything they were saying. "You guys need to slow down."

"Wait, *what*?" Soni said, holding up her hand. "You

mean to tell me you have no idea what you are?"

Mwikali shook her head frantically. "I have no clue what any of you are talking about. All I know is that I'm dangerous — probably even cursed — and that my sketchbook is, too."

Odwar smiled reassuringly as he handed the sketchbook back to Mwikali. "First of all, you're not dangerous. And second, you don't make things happen by drawing them. You're what's called a Seer — someone who's able to predict the future. So, your friend's sickness, the blizzard, even Mrs. Amdany turning into a monster — you didn't make any of those things happen. You just saw them in your mind before they did, and then drew them in your sketchbook. All you did was *predict* the future, not cause it to happen."

"And third," Xirsi cut in, "you're an Intasimi descendant. You come from a handful of special bloodlines, where every few hundred years, someone is born with a supernatural gift. Your bloodline is known for Seeing. That's why you're a Seer."

Mwikali arched an eyebrow. "Wait. Are you saying that I have a genetically inherited *superpower*?"

"You think just anyone can see into the future?" Soni asked, cocking her head.

Mwikali chewed on her bottom lip, staring at the grass

in front of her crossed legs. She had accurately predicted the future three times now. But still, *superpowers*? Things like that only happened in movies, right?

"You're not just a Seer, Mwikali," Xirsi said, throwing up his hands dramatically. "You're one of the rarest Seers in the world. You can see into the future like all the others can, but you also have the ability to see monsters in their true form. You have what's called 'sight beyond sight.' I've read about it before. Seers with sight beyond sight only come around once every *thousand* years."

"I know it's a lot to take in," Odwar said, noticing that Mwikali looked like a deer in the headlights. "We only found out that we were Intasimi descendants a few months ago. Mrs. Amdany is the first monster we've actually come face to face with. Well, we didn't see her true form like you did, but we sensed it. Anyway, all of this is pretty new to us, too."

Mwikali turned the information over in her head before suddenly perking up. "So, you guys have superpowers, too? Can I see?"

Soni held up her palm. "Chill. We don't know you like that."

Odwar placed a hand on Soni's shoulder. "Relax. She's Intasimi. Technically, she's one of us," he said.

"Technically," Soni stressed, under her breath.

Xirsi turned serious. "We keep all this a secret because people fear what they don't understand. There was a time when Intasimi descendants were hunted down and killed by people who were afraid of what they could do. Since then, our identities and powers have been kept a secret from the outside world."

He rose to his feet and flashed his huge, uneven smile. "Now, are you ready for some show and tell?"

Before she could answer, Xirsi lifted his head to the sky. His eyes, twinkling with excitement, darted around searching for something.

Suddenly, Mwikali heard the sound of birds chirping. It was distant at first, but then it grew louder and louder, until thousands of little birds appeared overhead.

Xirsi spread his arms wide and then brought one forward and made a swift cutting motion, as if he was doing karate. Slowly, the birds started to move around, organizing themselves. It took a second for Mwikali to realize what they were doing, but then she saw it. The birds had arranged themselves into letters. Letters that spelled out her name in the sky!

"*Ohmygosh*, that's so cool!" Mwikali gushed, unable to contain herself.

Xirsi took a bow. "All Intasimi bloodlines started off with one great ancestor whose powers got passed down through the generations. Our powers are similar to the ones our ancestors had, but not exactly the same. My Intasimi ancestor was called Gasara Winn. Ever heard of him?"

Mwikali shook her head, feeling embarrassed. "No, sorry."

"Well, Gasara Winn was a guardian of the forest," Xirsi said, continuing to wave his hands in the air. Now, he looked like he was conducting an orchestra. The birds responded dutifully in song and motion, chirping as they floated into all sorts of beautiful shapes and patterns.

"My people have always lived in the forest, but Gasara Winn did much more than just live there. He dedicated his life to protecting the trees and animals inside it. Somewhere along the way, that relationship turned magical. He began to commune with the trees and the wildlife in a way that nobody else could. He knew exactly what the forest needed and how to keep it healthy. And with birds, that relationship was even more special. They guided him, helped him understand what to do."

"But, how do you make them do..." Mwikali pointed to the sky, "...all of that?"

Xirsi chuckled. "It's hard to explain, but basically I can communicate with them telepathically."

"Can everyone in your family do that?" Mwikali asked,

suddenly wondering if her mom had superpowers, too.

"It doesn't work like that," Soni said, standing up. "These abilities are passed down through bloodlines, but not everyone gets them. Not everyone in the bloodline is an Intasimi descendant. The abilities skip generations, sometimes even disappear for hundreds of years at a time before reappearing."

Xirsi plopped down onto the floor as the birds dispersed. "So, it's unlikely that any other living member of your family is a Seer," he said, answering Mwikali's question unknowingly.

Soni intertwined her fingers and stretched out her arms. "My Intasimi ancestor was called Cierume. You've at least heard of *her*?"

Mwikali winced in response. This was getting really embarrassing.

Soni threw her head back and groaned. "*Girl!* Like, I get that you've lived outside of Kenya your entire life but, *hellooooo?* You've heard of the internet, right?"

"I know," Mwikali said, apologetically. It was becoming pitifully clear that she had a lot to learn about Kenyan history. "Just tell me about her. I'll research more later."

"Okay," Soni agreed, with an exasperated sigh. "So, Cierume was a totally fierce warrior. She led whole armies to victory at a time when girls weren't even allowed to fight! Hashtag Girl Power. What's even crazier is that she used a dancing stick on the battlefield instead of a spear! That's why they called her the dancing warrior. How cool is *that*? Anyway, when she fought, it was like she was performing one of her dances. It completely mesmerized her enemies and while they were all goo-goo eyed, she kicked their butts."

Mwikali's face glazed over in wonder. "So, I'm guessing that your superpower has something to do with dancing?"

"Kind of. As powers are passed down, they evolve and change to fit the new Intasimi descendant." Soni pulled out a pair of earplugs from her pocket and popped them into her ears. A playful glimmer lit up her eyes as she pointed to a rock resting on the ground. "Watch," she said.

Mwikali swiveled her head back and forth eagerly between the rock and Soni. At first, nothing happened — the rock remained perfectly still while Soni stood quietly with her eyes closed.

Then, Soni started to bob her head. Her movements were slight at first, but then she got more and more into it until she was headbanging like a rockstar.

Mwikali stole a glance at the rock — still nothing.

Suddenly, Soni opened her eyes and thrust her hand forward. The rock went flying through the air, blasted down the field by an invisible force. It landed on the ground with a heavy thud several feet away.

Mwikali clapped her hands in awe. "That's AH-mazing!"

Soni beamed as she took out her earplugs. "I struggled to control it at first, but I'm much better now. The earplugs help me focus on the imaginary drum beats playing in my head. I channel that sound into generating shockwaves through my hands."

"Powers awaken differently for different people," Odwar said, as he replaced Soni in the show and tell spot. "It sounds like your sketchbook triggered your power, probably because it means a lot to you."

Mwikali thought about how attached she was to her sketchbook. It made sense that it was the one thing that had awakened her superpower.

"Okay, so I'm guessing you've never heard of Luanda Magere. He was my Intasimi ancestor," Odwar said.

He stated it as a fact rather than a question, and Mwikali couldn't help but feel a sharp pang of disappointment. Her cluelessness was obvious to everyone.

Odwar carried on enthusiastically, completely

unaware of how much his words had stung. "Luanda Magere was known for being an invincible warrior. Spears and arrows would literally bounce off him. It was almost as if he was made of stone. The only way to hurt him was through his shadow."

"So, what, you're some sort of invincible stoneman?" Mwikali asked, half-jokingly.

Odwar grinned. "Not quite. Look at the ground," he said, before stuffing his hands into his pockets.

Mwikali stared at the ground, but all she could see was the spiky grass in the field. She was about to ask him what she was supposed to be looking at when she saw his shadow move. It was jumping up and down with arms flailing all over the place.

Ordinarily, there would have been nothing weird about a moving shadow, except for the fact that Odwar was standing completely still. His shadow was moving, but he wasn't!

"Are you controlling it?" Mwikali asked, fascinated.

"Sort of," he answered, scratching the back of his head. "My shadow is like my better half — my braver half. It does things I want to do or need to do, but that I'm afraid to."

Mwikali's head felt like it was about to explode. "This is all... This is a *lot*," she mumbled. "I don't know what to do with any of this."

"Well," Odwar said, dropping down beside her. "Now, you have a decision to make. You could choose to ignore your gift of Seeing and bury it inside you. If you do that, your power will eventually go away. You won't be a Seer anymore. You'll go back to being a completely normal kid."

"A completely *basic* kid," Soni snorted.

"Or you could choose to keep your gift," Odwar continued. "Our ancestors were given these powers so they could help people. That's what we're going to do: use our powers for good. We're not quite sure how yet — we're still learning them and all — but we're gonna try. You're welcome to try with us."

"Like Odwar said," Xirsi chipped in, "it's a use it or lose it situation. If you use your powers, you get to keep them. If you don't, you lose them."

"Yup. You're either in or out," Soni concluded, crossing her arms.

They turned to look at her, anticipating a speedy response.

But all Mwikali could do was bite her bottom lip. She grazed her fingers over her name on the cover of her sketchbook, considering the huge decision she had to make. Her whole life, she had been different — the new kid, the kid who didn't belong anywhere, the so-called freak. This was the year she was supposed to get away from all of that. She was supposed to have a new beginning as a regular kid. Accepting her power would mean giving up the dream of a normal life.

At the same time, Mwikali felt ready to discover what it was that made her so different. She was tired of burying whatever it was inside her. Tired of — what had Babu called it? — watering herself down to make other people feel more comfortable.

She puffed out her chest as the answer came to her — lifted her chin as she made the decision to stop hiding and start being her true self.

"I'm in," she said.

The ~~Crazy~~ Extraordinary Girl

DRIIIIIIIIIIIIING!

They all jumped, then relaxed. It was just the school bell. Morning break was over, but instead of going back to class, all students were required to report to the quad for Clubs' Parade.

Mwikali had read about the parade in the school brochure. It was an exhibition for all the school clubs, where they tried to recruit new members. It only happened once a year, at the end of the first week of school.

"There's one more thing," Mwikali said, suddenly remembering her encounter with Mrs. Amdany. "Back in the Lost and Found closet, Mrs. Amdany told me that something was coming. Something I wouldn't be able to stop. What did she mean by that?"

While Soni and Odwar exchanged blank stares, Xirsi's eyebrows bunched together. "Maybe she was just trying to creep you out?"

Mwikali paused to think about it. "Maybe. I dunno. She was definitely trying to scare me, I know that for sure."

"It's probably nothing," Soni said, standing up. "Anyway, I have to go. I'm minding the tent for Dance Club at the parade. Laters!" She turned and started to jog in the direction of the quad.

Xirsi jumped up, too. "Same. I'm running the Wildlife Club tent. See you!"

Mwikali and Odwar said goodbye to them as they sprinted up the field, and then followed slowly behind.

"Have you picked a club to join yet?" Odwar asked.

Mwikali nodded, distractedly. She was still trying to process everything that had happened in the past hour. Seeing a monster, learning she had a superpower, seeing a bunch of kids do out-of-this-world stuff... It felt like she had been pulled out of her body and was watching all of it from somewhere else, like a movie.

"Hey," Odwar said, giving her a concerned look. "It's going to be okay. You'll get used to the whole superpower thing. Just give it time."

She managed a weak smile, which seemed to flatten out some of the lines on his forehead.

"Come with me. I'll show you around the Clubs' Parade," he said. He started to dig around in his pocket. When he brought his hand out, he was holding a small plastic badge with the word "Prefect" written on it.

It snapped Mwikali right out of her thoughts. "Don't tell me you're one of *them*," she groaned.

He gave her a surprised look as he pinned the badge to his chest. "One of who?"

"The prefects, like Charo," she said, pretending to gag.

Odwar shook his head violently. "I am nothing like that guy. He thinks he's royalty just because his dad is the Chief Justice and President of the Supreme Court."

Mwikali nodded. Politicians and judges in Kenya were treated like royalty. It made sense that some of their kids would think they actually were. "What do prefects do, anyway?"

He waved his hand dismissively. "Prefects are just regular students who are given extra responsibilities. Like making sure everyone does what they're supposed to when the teacher isn't around. Reporting kids who break the rules, stuff like that."

"You rat out other kids?" Mwikali asked, pretending to gag again.

Odwar chuckled. "I try not to." He pointed at his badge. "This was my dad's idea. And by idea, I mean that Dad met with Babu one morning and a few minutes later, I was announced as a prefect. My dad's really into appearances and stuff. He wants me to become a County Representative like him one day. He's from Kisumu, where there are loads of unusually ambitious men."

They arrived at the quad to find it looking completely different from the way it did earlier. It now had white tents placed all around its perimeter, each labeled with the name of a different school club.

A large "Welcome to the Clubs' Parade!" sign pointed out where to start, and the two began to make their way around the crowded space. They had to squeeze past dozens of students as they walked. Some kids were just hanging out with old club friends while others were actively shopping around for new clubs to join. Everyone seemed to know Odwar and they had to keep stopping as kid after kid came up to say hi to him. He definitely was Mr. Popular.

Mwikali couldn't help but notice the pointed stares and giggles from some of her classmates. Her outburst in class was clearly still fresh in their minds. She shrank into herself and kept her eyes focused on the ground.

Odwar noticed and nudged her gently. "Don't worry about them. They'll forget about it soon enough. Besides, you saved us from that surprise quiz."

Mwikali nodded, grateful for his attempt to make her feel better.

The Young Farmers tent was the first in the exhibition and a blond-haired boy holding a fluffy black rabbit rushed over to greet them.

"Hey Odwar, and hellooo..." his voice trailed off as he searched in vain for Mwikali's name tag. "Hello, *new student*. Young Farmers club is a—" He was interrupted by the rowdy clucking of hens as they tried to break out of the makeshift chicken coop.

"Hey! Someone fasten that gate!" the boy called out, starting to run back towards the tent. "Young Farmers club is a great club," he yelled over his shoulder. "Please consider joining it!"

Mwikali giggled as she watched him and his club mates chasing after runaway chickens. There was no way she was joining Young Farmers. She was still traumatized from the time her mom had forced her to milk a cow on a visit to the Kenyan countryside. She had squealed a little too loudly and the cow had backed up, kicked over her stool, and sent her flying into a heap of cow poop. She had scrubbed her hands for two hours straight trying to get the stink off.

"Where's your name tag, by the way? Aren't all new students supposed to wear them for the first week?" Odwar asked, once they were walking again.

Mwikali told him about the incident with Babu earlier that week and how he had convinced her not to shorten her name if she didn't want to. She hadn't bothered to replace her name tag after she had ripped it off.

"Yeah, Xirsi got the same speech when he tried to spell his name with an H instead of an X."

"Wait. Xirsi is spelled with an X?" Mwikali asked, puzzled.

"Yup. It's pronounced HER-si but it's actually spelled with an X. So, when Xirsi tried to spell it with an H, the way it's pronounced, Babu gave him a whole speech about holding onto tradition. He also tried to convince Soni to start using her full name — Muthoni — instead of her nickname, but you know how Soni is. She's going to do whatever she wants to do."

Mwikali hummed in agreement. "It's pretty annoying getting your name butchered all the time. Teachers at my last school kept reading my name as M-WHY-kali instead of M-WEE-kali."

The next tent was labeled Pumping Iron. Weights and dumbbells were scattered inside the tent. Every kid around there was dressed in sports gear and looked like an Olympic athlete. Two of them jumped up when they saw Odwar.

"BRO! Where were you during break? We looked for you everywhere!" one of them said, while the other shoveled handfuls of chevra into his mouth.

The smell of the sweet and spicy snack reminded

Mwikali of her mom. Mom loved to spoon the spicy fried lentils, chickpeas, peanuts and flaked rice directly into her mouth from the packet.

For a moment, she felt a twinge of sadness that she wouldn't be able to talk to her mom about everything she had just learned. I mean, how could she? Mom had pinned all her hopes on Mwikali having a fresh start and a normal childhood in Kenya. The events of the past few hours had been anything *but* normal. Her hands grew clammy at the thought of keeping a secret as big as this from her.

"Pole, guys. My bad. I had something I needed to do during break," Odwar told his friends. "Mwikali, these are my boys, Maina and Rohan. Guys, meet Mwikali."

"*Hiii Mwikaliii*," they teased, in high pitched voices.

Odwar rolled his eyes and stole the packet of chevra from Rohan who was waggling his eyebrows suggestively at the two of them.

The two boys must have been in a different Grade Six class because Mwikali hadn't noticed them in theirs during the week.

"Wait, is this the new girl? The one who..." Maina dropped his voice as he raised a forefinger to his head and made a swirling motion. The universal sign for crazy. Mwikali felt like she had been punched in the gut.

"The one who saved us from a quiz?" Odwar said, confidently. "Yup. Mwikali's performance was flawless. Mrs. Amdany was so mad that she rage quit and just bounced instead of giving us the quiz."

Maina and Rohan exchanged raised eyebrows and then turned to Mwikali with high-fives and pats on the back. She flashed a grateful smile at Odwar. He had actually convinced them that she had freaked out in class on purpose!

"Anyway, we need to keep it moving," Odwar said, ushering Mwikali away from them. "Let's play this afternoon," he added, twiddling his fingers on an imaginary gamepad. The two boys gave him thumbs up signs as they walked away.

Mwikali elbowed Odwar softly as they strolled. "Thanks for that."

He elbowed back. "No worries."

"So, I'm guessing that's your club? Pumping Iron?" Mwikali asked, changing the topic.

"I wish," he said, emptying the chevra packet into his mouth. "I wanted to join Pumping Iron, but my dad refused. He thinks it's dumb."

He pointed to the next tent labeled President's Award Scheme. "*This* is my club," he said glumly. "Another one of Dad's great ideas."

Rows of seats were set up inside the President's Award Scheme tent. They were filled with very serious-looking kids, all facing a speaker who stood at a lectern.

"Looks intense," Mwikali said, noticing how quiet and still everyone was inside.

Odwar sighed. "It is. It's all about developing leadership skills. You have to go through all these different levels until you finally get an award from the President. It's an okay club, I guess. It's just not me. I'm not into that kind of stuff and I just wish my dad respected that."

Mwikali felt sorry for him. It must have been hard having such a controlling dad. She'd never met her own dad, but having one like Odwar's sounded pretty bad.

They walked by the Wildlife Club next and spotted Xirsi talking animatedly to a group of kids while flipping through a nature photography book. He looked like he was really into it but stopped to quickly wave at them before returning to his captivated audience.

Seeing Xirsi reminded Mwikali of everything that had happened that morning. She felt a weight clamp down on her chest. What if she had made the wrong decision? What if she wasn't cut out for this supernatural gift thing?

"How was it for you guys when your powers

awakened?" she asked.

Odwar considered her question for a while. "It was pretty crazy. We were on our end-of-year school trip to the nature reserve. I guess we must have camped near a monster or something because all of a sudden my shadow started going ballistic — moving up, down, all around on its own. It was the first time that had happened, and I almost lost it. Xirsi was the only one who noticed what was happening to me, and he came running over and pointed to the sky. That's when I noticed hundreds of birds circling right above him. He was freaking out, too. Saying that he could hear the birds' thoughts — that they were scared.

"By this time, a group of kids had gathered to look at the birds. Luckily, they had crowded all around us and couldn't see my shadow moving. Soni was one of them. Xirsi and I were looking around to see if anyone else was feeling what we were when we saw how nervous Soni looked. We called her over. She stretched out her hand and our whole tent swayed, like it had been hit by a gust of wind. That's how it happened. That night we stayed up practicing and showing each other what we could do."

"You all awakened on the same day?"

Odwar nodded. "But what we didn't know was that someone had been watching us the entire time, waiting for it to happen. Now that I think about it, I'm guessing he took us to that specific campsite because he knew there was a monster nearby. He must have wanted the awakening to happen when he could help us through it. He's been like a mentor to us ever since. And he's the one who told us that you would be coming to our school this year."

The realization dawned on Mwikali. "*That's* why you guys were staring at me so much. And why you passed me that note. You already knew about me!"

Odwar chuckled. "Yeah. Our mentor — Mr. Lemayian — told us about you. He's a part-time History teacher and knows everything there is to know about the Intasimi bloodlines. He can tell which descendants will be gifted and which ones won't. He knew about Soni, Xirsi and me, and about you, too."

They stopped at the Arts & Crafts tent and Mwikali popped in to sign up. The best thing that had happened to her that day was learning that she wasn't cursed, and neither was her sketchbook. She didn't have to avoid drawing anymore! After that, it was a no-brainer which club she would join.

Once she'd registered for the club, they cruised by the Journalism and First Aid club tents before arriving at the last one, which was also the loudest. It belonged to the Dance Club. Nigerian afrobeat blasted from a speaker inside the tent, while genge music, which Auntie had described as a type of Kenyan hip hop, blared from a speaker on the outside.

Everywhere they looked, there were kids dancing. Soni was one of them and when they waved at her, she waved back mid-dance routine without missing a single beat. With her space buns, fitted school pants and stylish combat boots, she looked like she could have been in a music video.

They stood watching her for several minutes after the school bell rang. And they weren't the only ones. A crowd of kids from all over the quad soon formed around Soni to watch her dance. She was that good.

Mwikali's mind drifted as the performance went on. It was muddied from all the new information it needed to process. "What do twelve-year-old kids with supernatural abilities even do?" she muttered.

"Right now, our job is to learn," Odwar stated, confidently. "At least, that's what Mr. Lemayian always says. We need to understand more about our powers. That's where he comes in. We're supposed to have our first training session of the semester with him tomorrow. He made up a Saturday tutoring class just for that, for us. That includes you now. You have to come."

Mwikali scrunched up her face. "I dunno... I'll have to ask my Mum."

"I'm sure it'll be fine. Parents always say yes to school stuff, especially tutoring." Odwar glanced over at the parking lot. "My dad's driver is here. See you tomorrow. Class starts at 9."

He turned around to leave but then stopped short, grinning. "You know, we all knew you were coming and that you were a Seer, but the fact that you can see monsters in true form? That was totally unexpected. Who knew you'd be so extraordinary?"

Extraordinary? Mwikali's heart fluttered. Sure, extraordinary was just another word for different, but for the first time in her life, she found herself bursting with pride at her difference. For once, being called different made her feel more confident than ever.

"See you, Seer!" he repeated with a smile, before hustling toward the parking lot.

An unexpected joy took over Mwikali. Maybe this Intasimi descendant thing wasn't so bad after all. She'd learned something cool about herself, made new friends, and been reunited with her love of drawing. This might have been the craziest, best day of her entire life.

"Don't you go home in one of the school vans?" Xirsi asked, suddenly appearing beside her.

"Yeah. Why?"

His eyebrows went up. "*Uhhh*, because you should have been at your van like ten minutes ago when the bell rang?"

Mwikali's heart dropped. Why would she need school transport in the middle of the day? Wait, why was *Odwar* going home in the middle of the day?

"But it's not home time yet," Mwikali said, confused.

"Today is a half-day. Fridays are always half-days here. You didn't know that?"

It felt like the world around Mwikali was spinning as she started to run toward the school van pick-up area. Her emergency contact — Mom — wasn't yet back from her trip, phones weren't allowed in school so she couldn't call anybody else, and judging by the empty parking lot, most of the teachers had already left. She had no way of getting home if she got left by the van.

"You should be fine, though," Xirsi yelled, as he ran beside her. "Every van has an assigned prefect to check the roster and make sure nobody gets left behind. Who's your van prefect?"

Mwikali felt the panic rising in her throat as she remembered the words spoken to her earlier that week. "You'll regret this," he had said. She swallowed. "My van prefect is Charo!"

She skidded to a stop at the curb. There were three vans snaking around the roundabout in the center of the parking lot, gearing up to drive off. They all looked exactly the same. She couldn't tell which one was hers!

"What zone are you in?" Xirsi asked.

That's when she noticed the paper signs stuck to each of the windscreens with different numbers written on them. The three vans were labeled Zones 2, 4 and 5. Which one was hers? Her brain, already fuzzy from a crazy morning, was now completely fogged up. Was it Zone 2? 1?

"I don't remember!" Mwikali panted.

Xirsi grabbed her hand and pulled her toward the roundabout. He banged on the first van until the agitated driver rolled down his window.

"If you're not on the roster, you can't enter," he said gruffly.

"I don't know if I'm on it or not! I don't remember what zone I'm in!" Mwikali cried.

The driver, who looked completely unbothered, sighed. "Where do you live?"

"Iveti Estate," Mwikali said, quickly. At least she could remember that.

The driver pointed toward the school gate. "You're in Zone 3. There's your van."

Mwikali followed the driver's pointed finger to see a yellow van shooting out of the school gate. And when she looked closer, she saw Charo staring out of the back window with a satisfied grin smeared across his face.

The ~~Story~~ Legend

"Oh no, no, no!" Mwikali cried, as she watched her Zone 3 van turn into a small dot down the road and then disappear altogether.

"What's going on?" Soni asked, joining them in the parking lot.

"She missed her van," Xirsi said, matter-of-factly. "But her estate is close by. I can take you home, Mwikali."

Mwikali clutched her chest. "You will? Thanks!" she exhaled.

"I'll come with you guys. My dad said he'd be late 'cuz of work. I'd rather wait for him at your place than here. I mean, if that's okay?"

"Totally," Mwikali said. It would be fun to have a friend over, and it would give her a chance to find out more about the whole Intasimi thing.

With Xirsi leading the way, they walked through the Savanna Academy parking lot. Mwikali expected them to hop into a waiting car at any minute and it wasn't until they were approaching the school gate that she wondered if she had misunderstood him.

"The matatu I take home passes by your neighborhood," Xirsi said, casually. "Put your sketchbook inside your bag. Nairobi is nicknamed 'Nairobbery' for a reason. Make sure you hang on tight to your stuff once we're on the main road, sawa?"

Mwikali managed to squeak out a soft "Okay" in return but, in truth, she was far from okay. She was actually trying hard not to let her intense fear of matatus show. She had seen the colorfully decorated minibuses hurtling down the roads before, and they looked absolutely terrifying. Not only were they always jam packed to the point where some people had to hang out of the door, but they were also driven really, really fast.

Her heart jumped at the mere thought of riding in one now. Still, she squeezed the straps of her backpack and followed Xirsi out onto the main road. She was going to have to face her fear if she wanted to get home.

When they got to the road, Xirsi stretched out his hand and waved it in the direction of oncoming traffic. Almost immediately, a matatu appeared out of nowhere, veered off the road, and then came hurtling down the sidewalk toward them.

Mwikali staggered backward and then coughed up dust when it stopped only inches away from her feet. It was crammed with passengers. A couple of them straddled the door, with half their bodies swinging out of the open vehicle.

Nope. There was no way she was getting into that death trap. There had to be another way to get home. She turned to Xirsi and then to Soni, shaking her head and mouthing the word "No."

Soni looped her arm through Mwikali's, pulling her forward as she marched towards the matatu. "You'll be just fine, princess," she teased.

One of the men, who was leaning out of the door, quickly jumped out and beckoned for them to get in. He hastened the process by shoving them into the first row of seats. Then, he hopped back in and gave the side of the matatu two hard slaps. The whole thing happened so quickly that, before Mwikali knew it, she was squished inside the matatu and speeding down the road.

Xirsi gave her a thumbs up while Soni grinned, amused. It was just about all they could do since the deafening R&B music blasting from surround sound speakers inside the matatu made talking impossible. Mwikali tried to force out a brave chuckle but ended up choking on the stuffy air, heavy with the smells of sweaty armpits, exhaust fumes, and the French fries someone was eating in the back.

She strained her head toward the nearest window and

rejoiced when a tiny stream of fresh air reached her nose. *She could do this.* All she needed was to keep her face in the direct pathway of that breeze. And try not to think about the burly man who kept nodding off onto her shoulder...

Mwikali further distracted herself by focusing on the passing scenery as they sped along. She spotted several shops and restaurants along the way — some familiar and others that she had never seen before — and made a note of all the ones she and Mom could try during their weekly mommy-daughter dates.

Several minutes into the ride, the matatu driver sucked his teeth and muttered a slew of curses under his breath. An instant later, Mwikali saw why. A policeman was motioning for them to pull over to the side of the road.

There always seemed to be police officers out on the streets in Nairobi. And they never seemed happy. This one was no exception. His round face glistened with sweat as he pointed angrily at the matatu driver who had obediently brought the vehicle to a stop beside him.

Mwikali couldn't make out what the policeman was saying over the music, but whatever the matatu driver said back was enough to send the officer flying into a rage.

Xirsi tapped Mwikali's knee and then pointed up. "Something isn't right," he whispered breathlessly, his nose already beaded with sweat.

Mwikali looked at Soni's nodding face, and then up to the sky where she saw a whirlwind of birds circling the air just above the matatu. And when she looked back down at the police officer, she understood why.

He wasn't human anymore.

The first thing she noticed was the color of his face. It had turned bright green. Then, his eyes — they were now a pair of black, gaping holes, just like Mrs. Amdany's. His nose was noticeably larger too, with a heavy bullring dangling beneath flared nostrils. Finally, two large, sharp, lower canine teeth jutted out of his drooling mouth.

He was an ogre. A real life ogre.

Mwikali's breathing quickened and she squeezed her eyes shut, unable to stand the nightmare in front of her.

"What is it?" Soni rasped. "What do you see?"

She tried to steady her breathing enough to speak. "The cop. He's an...an ogre."

Xirsi jolted in surprise. "You mean like...*Shrek?*"

"No, not like Shrek! Evil-eyed, drooling, and very, very scary!" Mwikali whimpered.

Xirsi stuck his head out of the window and then

ducked back in. "Okay, you can't let him know that you can see his true form, sawa? It might make him mad, like it did Mrs. Amdany."

Mwikali covered her face with her hands. Beside her, Xirsi kept muttering "Calm down" over and over again. She wasn't sure if he was talking to her or to his birds. Soni, on the other hand, kept squeezing Mwikali's arm and whispering — maybe to herself — that it would be over soon.

And it was. Eventually, the policeman's growls died down and then changed back into a regular human voice. He even broke into a loud laugh. The matatu driver had somehow managed to calm him down.

Mwikali cracked an eye open and peeped out. He was human again! Both he and Mrs. Amdany had gone from looking like monsters to looking normal in the flash of an eye.

"He's back to normal," Mwikali said, blowing out a breath.

As the matatu got back on the road, Xirsi asked Mwikali to describe exactly what the ogre had looked like. He couldn't stop shaking his head in fascination as she spoke.

"It looks like their true forms come out when they're angry," he said, thoughtfully. "Like, they're too emotional to keep their monster-sides hidden."

Mwikali had just opened her mouth to agree when Soni slammed her hand against the side of the matatu.

"Shukisha!" she shouted, and a second later, they swerved to the side of the road, coming to a stop right outside the Iveti Estate gate.

In the same lightning quick way they had been bundled into the matatu, they were bundled out, with Xirsi barely able to shout a quick "Bye!" to them before the vehicle sped off.

Mwikali led Soni to her house, checking the driveway to see if Mom was back from her trip yet. She wasn't.

"Hi, Auntie!" Mwikali called out, as they walked into the living room.

Auntie appeared at the door to the kitchen with confusion written all over her face. "Ai, Mwikali? What are you doing home?"

Mwikali shrugged. "Fridays are half-days. Nice, eh? I don't think Mom knew."

"Oh, okay," Auntie said. "And you've come with a friend?"

"Yeah, this is Soni."

Soni waved. "Hi, Mwikali's Auntie."

"Hi, Soni. You girls are just in time for lunch," Auntie said, walking back into the kitchen.

"It smells yummy," Soni replied, following closely behind.

On Fridays, Auntie cooked all the food they would eat over the weekend. She made different meat stews, boiled rice, prepped the potatoes for Friesday aka Friday night dinner and sometimes, when she felt like it, she'd add something special to the menu, like she had that day.

She hummed as she loaded their plates with food. "I made chapatis and goat stew. Very yummy," Auntie boasted, as she spooned enough food to feed two grown men.

"Make sure you finish," she commanded, handing over the dishes.

"We will!" Soni called over her shoulder, as they climbed the stairs to Mwikali's room.

Their meal turned out to be even yummier than it smelled. The goat meat was tender and bursting with flavor. The chapatis — perfectly soft and layered.

Before long, Soni was mopping up the remaining soup from her plate with her last piece of flatbread. "Your auntie is a good cook!" she gushed.

Mwikali nodded as she collected their empty dishes and stacked them on her desk. "Yeah, she's the best." She grabbed her cell phone from her nightstand and switched it on. "Here, you can call your dad."

A few minutes later, Soni hung up. "He'll be here in, like, an hour."

"Can I ask you something?" Mwikali inquired as they settled on the bed. "You said that you've gotten better at using your power... How? I mean, what have you been doing to get better at it?"

"The biggest thing, besides just practicing whenever I can, has been learning more about my family history and my Intasimi ancestor. Learning about who they were, how they lived, how they used their powers...stuff like that."

"How do I find out who my Intasimi ancestor was? Wait, let me guess, the internet?" Mwikali asked, with a half-smile.

Soni laughed. "Yup, the internet is definitely your friend when it comes to finding out a bunch of this stuff. But, I already know who she was. Your Intasimi ancestor was none other than the great prophetess, Syokimau."

Soni paused, waiting for a hint of recognition to show on Mwikali's face. When it didn't, Soni picked up a pillow and whacked her over the head with it. "C'mon! Not even *her*? There are towns and railway stations literally named after her... Huge bronze Syokimau statues made in her image, even!"

"Geez, I said I was sorry! I'll do better," Mwikali cried.

She was laughing while rubbing her head where the pillow had made impact.

"You better," Soni threatened, shaking the pillow in the air. "Anyway, Mr. Lemayian — Odwar probably told you about him — told us that you were related to Syokimau on your dad's side."

Mwikali's heart dropped into the pit of her stomach. Her dad's side? She didn't know anything about that side of her family. How could she? Dad had walked out on them when she was still an infant.

"Oh," Soni said quietly, noticing her reaction. "Is he... not around?"

Mwikali sighed. "Nope. So I guess it's all up to the internet, then." She fired up her laptop and typed the name "Syokimau" into the search bar.

The search pulled up a bunch of myths and historical accounts. And with Soni's help, Mwikali was able to piece together the story — the legend — of her great ancestor.

Syokimau's beginnings were a mystery, her parents unknown. She was simply discovered tucked inside a hollowed out Mugumo tree when she was an infant. Nobody knew where she had come from.

Her gift for predicting the future began at an early age and she soon grew to become one of the most accurate Seers in history. She saved her people from enemy attacks countless times by predicting when and how they would happen.

Syokimau even made a prophecy about the arrival of the colonizers, decades before they first set foot in Kenya. In her vision, Syokimau had seen people with skin like meat (Soni explained that these were colonizers) who carried fire in their pockets (matchboxes) and spoke a language that sounded like gibberish (English). She said that these people would be carried around by a long snake that belched smoke (a train). She also warned that they would bring death and destruction.

Every single thing that Syokimau predicted later came true. European colonizers did eventually arrive in Kenya. To the locals, their sunburned skin looked like the pink flesh of animal meat and, when they spoke, they did so in a language that sounded like nonsense. The fact that they built a railroad system and travelled around with matchboxes in their pockets, further proved that Syokimau's predictions had been accurate.

"Wow," Mwikali said, when they were done. "Syokimau helped her community in every way she could, right up until she grew old and died. I can't believe I'm related to someone who was so awesome."

Soni nodded so hard that her space buns bounced up and down. "Yeah! And Mr. Lemayian can fill you in on anything else you need to know about her. You can ask him about it tomorrow. You're coming for Saturday tutoring, right?"

"I think so. But I need to ask my—"

The sound of metal scraping against concrete interrupted her.

" —Mom. I think that's her right now," Mwikali said. She hopped off the bed and peered out of the window. "Yup! My auntie is opening the gate for her. Looks like she brought home a friend from work, too."

As a senior flight attendant, Mom would sometimes invite younger trainees home with her. She said it was all part of making them feel less homesick on their first long trip. They would usually come over for the afternoon and then leave right after dinner.

Mwikali's mom pulled her into a bear hug as soon as she walked in. "*Mwikaliii*, I missed you so much! How was your first week of school? And who's this? You've made friends already? I knew you'd have a much easier time at this school—"

"I missed you too, Mom," Mwikali said quickly, cutting her off before she could say any more. "This is Soni. Her dad is picking her up later."

Soni got a big hug of her own before Mom finally introduced the woman standing beside her as Molly, a junior trainee on her first trip. Molly's hair was big as a blimp and she wore a glossy layer of pink lipstick all over her plumped-up lips.

"Oh, bless your hearts, aren't y'all just the cutest little things? With your itty bitty school uniforms! How old are you?" Molly drawled.

Soni stuck out her chin and crossed her arms. "We're both twelve and in sixth grade."

Molly's mouth widened in surprise. "Well, I'll be! You speak so well!"

"So do you!" Soni said, imitating the woman's heavy southern accent. Mwikali's mom burst out laughing as Molly's eyebrows knitted together in confusion.

"You girls can go back upstairs. Soni, I'll let you know when your dad gets here."

They giggled all the way up the stairs. "That response was perfect!" Mwikali wheezed, once they were back in her room. "I'm stealing that for the next time one of Mom's work friends says something dumb. One time? This Bulgarian dude asked us if Africans lived in trees and kept lions as pets!"

Soni rolled her eyes. "Are you serious? UGH!" She shook her head and then gave Mwikali a meaningful look. "What your Mom said earlier, about things being better for you now that you've switched schools... I'm guessing you had problems at your last school? After you predicted your friend getting sick?"

Mwikali dropped her eyes to the floor. She opened her mouth to speak — to explain — but no words came out. All she could do was shuffle her feet.

"You don't have to say anything," Soni said, reaching out to squeeze her hand. "The reason it takes me a while to warm up to people — the reason I can be kind of intense — is because something like that happened to me, too. Someone found out about my gift and...it was bad. That's why I don't trust people so easily. Anyway, you don't have to be embarrassed about it. I get it. I've been there."

"Thanks." Mwikali's voice was thick with emotion, her eyes moist. "I guess I'm not totally over it yet. The whole thing made me feel like I was too weird to belong anywhere or with anyone."

Soni squeezed her hand even tighter. "Well, now you've met us. And we're all *super* weird. We can all belong to each other."

The Tutoring
~~Session~~ Fail

Mr. Lemayian was nothing like Mwikali had expected. She had pictured a small, grumpy man with a balding head and a love of gray half-sweaters. In her mind, mentors were old and crabby. The real Mr. Lemayian, however, turned out to be the complete opposite.

In reality, he was tall and youthful looking, with a broad chest and a head full of ruby red locs that reached all the way down to his waist. He was the kind of person who moved his hands excitedly while he talked, and when Mwikali met him on that first Saturday, he wore stacks of colorful beaded bracelets on his wrist that rapped against each other every time he moved.

He jogged up to the car and cheerfully introduced himself as soon as Mwikali and her mom pulled up to the school parking lot.

"It's so nice to meet you, Mr. Lemayian!" Mom said, sticking her hand out of the driver's side window to shake his. "Mwikali couldn't be more excited about this tutoring class. She's never woken up this early on a Saturday in her life!"

The truth was that Mwikali hadn't slept at all. She had been up all night, staring at the ceiling and replaying the events of her chaotic day. Most of all, she had spent the night trying to bury the seeds of doubt that had sprouted inside her. What if she wasn't cut out for this superpower stuff? What if she couldn't actually predict the future, and every other time had been a fluke?

Mwikali had wrestled with her thoughts and fears all through the night. And by the time the sky brightened, she had decided to tell her mom everything — that monsters were real, that she was an Intasimi descendant, and that she was a Seer. She needed one of Mom's pep talks. She needed to hear that everything was going to be okay, now more than ever.

But that morning, Mom had been over the moon about Mwikali "settling in so well". She had practically leaped into the air with joy when Mwikali had told her about being invited to a tutoring session. She had just kept going on and on about how happy she was that Mwikali would finally get to have a "happy, normal childhood experience." It would have broken her heart to hear anything else, so Mwikali had kept her mouth shut.

Mom's eyes gleamed with joy as she spoke to Mr. Lemayian. "I even forgot to ask what subject you'll be tutoring! Is it Swahili? I know Mwikali needs a lot of help with that," she babbled.

He gave her an easy smile and clapped his hands together. "Well, Mama Mwikali, I tutor the kids in whichever area they need help with the most."

"Great. That's great. I'm just so happy that she's found friends and a club and—"

"Mom!" Mwikali interrupted, opening the car door. "I'll see you at lunch time. Love you, bye!"

Mwikali watched as her mom smiled and dabbed at the corners of her eyes while backing the car up. It was a good thing she had decided to keep her secret. Mom was more desperate for her to fit in and have a normal life than she had realized.

"The others are already here," Mr. Lemayian announced, as they walked. "I'm happy to finally meet you. I've been told you had quite an exciting day yesterday."

Mwikali had to jog to keep up with his giant strides. "Yeah, it was insane."

He came to an abrupt stop and turned to face her. "I just want you to know that I'm here to help. I know that this is all a big change for you. And change can be scary. If you're struggling with anything, anything at all, please let me know."

Mwikali twisted her mouth. Sighed. "What if... What

if I can't actually do this and I'm not really a Seer? What if this is all just a big fluke? Or a one-time thing that never happens again?"

Mr. Lemayian placed one hand on her shoulder. The other moved around as he talked. "This is no mistake. You are the direct descendant of the great Seer Syokimau. Her spirit burns in you. Her gift flows through your veins. And there's something else... Come, the others need to hear this as well."

They sat close to the front of the Six Chui classroom while Mr. Lemayian leaned back against the teacher's desk. "Now that Mwikali is here, there's something I've been meaning to tell you. I realized it as soon as I read Mwikali's admission file and found out who she was." He paused and took a breath. "The four of you are not just Intasimi descendants. You're much more than that. You're a miracle. One that I didn't think I'd ever live to see."

He walked up so that he was right in front of them, and then leaned in. "Very few people get the supernatural gifts you kids have. I mean, it's rare enough to have more than one Intasimi heir living at the same time as another. But to have four? All the same age? It's unheard of. A miracle."

Mwikali glanced at the other three and was relieved

to see that they were just as confused as she was. This information was new to them, too.

"Back in the olden days, young men were grouped into age sets and trained to fight," Mr. Lemayian continued. "They believed that children who were around the same age had a unique bond — one that made them stronger when they fought side by side. You four are a perfect age set of supernaturally gifted children. That means that you're destined not just to be Intasimi descendants, but Intasimi Warriors."

For a few seconds, nobody said a word. Mwikali started to feel dizzy, her ears blocked. *Warriors?* She was no warrior! This had to be some sort of mistake. Thankfully, the others spoke up before she had to.

Xirsi was first. "Warriors? Nah, Mr. Lemayian. I'm a man of science. I'm not a soldier."

Soni bobbed her head up and down in agreement. "We literally only found out about our powers the other day. There's *no way* we're ready for war."

"And war against who? Monsters like Mrs. Amdany? We're definitely not ready for that," Odwar added.

"You may not have a choice!" Mr. Lemayian said, throwing up his hands. "You told me that Mrs. Amdany warned that something was coming. Guess what? She wasn't bluffing. I can feel it too. A great evil is on its way, and the world will need the Intasimi Warriors to save it when the time comes."

"You want us to save the world?" Mwikali asked, her voice no more than a whisper.

"I want you to try," Mr. Lemayian answered. "And I'm going to do everything I can to help you. That's what our tutoring sessions are for — to prepare you for whatever you may have to face."

Before any of them had a chance to protest any further, he pulled down the screen projector in front of the blackboard and tapped the keys on his laptop. "Our Saturday classes will be split into two. First up: Intasimi history, because you need to know about the past in order to prepare for the future. And then: power practice, so you can better understand, and therefore use, your powers."

Mr. Lemayian thrust a pointed finger at the screen where an image of a tall, bald woman had just appeared. She was dressed in animal skins, with a small gourd hanging from her waist.

"For today's history class, we'll focus on Syokimau, in honor of the newest member of our group. This is the only drawing of her that has survived to date. You see the gourd? It was filled with medicinal herbs. She carried it around with her, helping the sick wherever she went. You see, Syokimau was not just a Seer; she was a medicine woman, too. She used her gift to help her people in every way she could, by seeing what hidden diseases ailed them or warning them when trouble was in their futures. She used her gifts in service of her people, every time she could. That's what being a warrior is about. Don't think of it as fighting the enemy. Think of it as serving the people."

He went on to tell them how Syokimau would get visions in her dreams. Visions that were so clear that she could see, hear, touch, smell and taste everything in them. He also told them that great Seers could see into the past as well as the future. They had the power to see both what *had* happened and what *would* happen.

Mwikali leaned forward and teetered on the edge of her seat as Mr. Lemayian described how Syokimau had died not once, but three times. Each time, her people had mourned her death and then laid her body out in the forest, as was the custom in those days. Each time, she had been found wandering a few days later, her old body full of new life. On the third and final time, she had been found in the usual spot and in the position she used to talk to the ancestors. That time, they had welcomed her into the afterworld, for good.

Mr. Lemayian explained that Seeing was a powerful

gift, especially for Seers like her with sight beyond sight who could see things even other Seers couldn't, like monsters in true form. He revealed that Seers could develop other powers too, like being able to sense intuitively what someone was about to do or whether they were telling the truth.

He also warned her that there were some weaknesses that came with being a Seer. "Seeing isn't like asking a mirror on the wall or a magic 8-ball to give you an answer. The visions will seek you out, and you have no control over what they'll be. Sometimes you'll be able to stop bad things from happening; sometimes you won't. Your job is to do your best. To help whenever you can."

After Intasimi history, they split up for power practice. Xirsi and Odwar went to the sports field where both abundant sun and birds could be found. Soni went to find an empty classroom where it was quiet enough for her to focus. And Mwikali remained behind, staring at a blank page in her sketchbook.

Twenty minutes later, the page was still blank. It was like she had artist's block or something. She tried to draw, but nothing came to her.

"Relax and don't worry about it," Mr. Lemayian said encouragingly. "Like I said, the visions will find you. Just like they did before."

Not a single vision found her that Saturday, nor the one that followed, nor the one after that. And four Saturdays later, Mwikali's sketchbook was still blank, as if both her artist's brain and her Seeing brain were blocked.

While her friends got better at controlling their powers, she felt like she was letting everyone down. Sooner or later, they would realize that she would never be ready to save the world, no matter how many tutoring sessions she attended.

The only thing that kept her going was how supportive Mr. Lemayian and her friends were. They refused to give up on her, and so she refused to give up on herself. At least, not yet.

There was also the history portion of class, which quickly became the highlight of her week. She learned all sorts of cool things about the Intasimi bloodlines, Kenyan culture, and the different types of monsters that existed.

Mrs. Amdany was apparently a shiqq — a type of half-formed beast. Monsters like her were cunning and deceitful, often using their intellect and powers of persuasion to get things done their way. Many shiqqs became politicians, celebrities, cult leaders.

Ogres, on the other hand, were more aggressive. They

used brute force and money (if they had any) to get their hands on what they wanted. Like all other monsters, they too were drawn to positions of power, so they became police officers, business tycoons, professional athletes and things of that sort.

But by far the biggest bonus of the Saturday sessions was hanging out with Soni, Odwar, and Xirsi. All four had become the closest of friends, both in and out of school.

She and Soni spent their weekday evenings together, with Soni's dad picking her up from her house every day after school. And thanks to Odwar and his popularity, nobody had said another word to her about what happened in Mrs. Amdany's class. Being seen with him had earned her a lifetime's worth of street cred with the other kids. Even Charo kept his distance from her and made sure the van waited for her when she was late. While the other two were doing dance or prefect related stuff, Mwikali and Xirsi would huddle together trading details on all the cool Intasimi- or monster-related stuff they found on the internet.

Everything was going well. Everything except for Mwikali's power to see. That had been M.I.A. for almost a month.

"Should we start making random people mad? Try

and get them into monster mode? See if you've still got it?" Xirsi joked.

Odwar punched him in the arm before turning to Mwikali. "Or maybe all the monsters have disappeared and there's nothing important happening in the future. There's nothing to see."

"What I know is, the more you stress, the less the chance that you'll come out of this superpower block, or whatever it is. You need to chill," Soni said, throwing an arm around Mwikali.

"But what if... What if my ability only kicks in when I'm freaking out about something? What if the only way I can be a Seer is if I'm scared? Or miserable? Guys, I don't want to have a miserable life!"

"I have another idea," Xirsi started.

Odwar raised a balled fist in warning. "Bro, if you say we should find the ogre-cop and make him mad..."

"No, not that," Xirsi said, chuckling. "Over the holiday, I went to my shagz — the village where my dad, granddad, great granddad, and all my ancestors are from. And when I was there, especially when I was around my family, it was like I could hear the birds more clearly. Like my powers got a boost just by being around them. Maybe... Maybe you could try that."

Soni made the sound a buzzer makes when someone

gives the wrong answer. "Not gonna work. She has zero contact with her dad. How would she even begin to find her shagz?"

"Wait, I think Xirsi's onto something," Mwikali said, stroking her chin. "Learning about my dad and his people, getting closer to that part of my history... That might be the missing link — the thing that fully connects me to my power."

She bit her lower lip and sighed. "I know who I need to talk to. And she's not going to like it. At all."

The ~~Talk~~ Picture

Robert. That was his name. And that was all Mwikali knew about him. It was all Mom would tell her, the few times she had dared to ask.

She was only six years old the first time she had questioned her mom about her father. But even then, she had noticed how her mom's face had hardened, and had wondered if she'd done something wrong by asking where he was, why he didn't live with them.

That day, Mom had stared out onto the road for a while and then sighed before answering. "Your father left when you were a baby. He wasn't ready to be a dad." With that, she had turned the car radio on and rolled down the window to let even more noise in. The discussion was over.

A couple of years later, when she had been told to draw a family tree for a homework assignment, Mom had given her his name — Robert. At first, she had pretended not to hear Mwikali's question. Then she had told her to leave that part of the tree blank. But Mwikali had insisted and, eventually, Mom had given in.

"Write 'Robert.' That's his name."

Mwikali had scribbled the name onto her tree, smiling triumphantly after successfully drawing out this new piece of information. But her joy had been cut short when, out of the corner of her eye, she had seen Mom knuckle a stream of tears away. She had felt horrible, and had never asked about him again.

But now, as she said goodbye to her friends and climbed into the car after her fourth tutoring class, she knew that she had no choice. She had to find out more about her dad — about Robert — if she was going to break through her block and become the Seer everyone seemed to think she was meant to be.

So, on the ride back home, Mwikali worked up her courage and practiced what she was going to say. Xirsi had suggested a lengthy explanation of how important knowing family history was. It began with research on how health history in particular could help prevent genetic disorders, and ended with a Marcus Garvey quote that said not knowing your past was like being a tree without roots.

Soni had told her to demand to know about her dad. She said it was Mwikali's "God-given right" to know who he was.

Odwar had advised her not to beat around the bush.

She should just ask the question. No explanation or anything.

Mwikali took in all of her friends' advice and then later, when she and her mom were watching TV together in the living room, she went for it in her own way.

"Mom, I know you don't like to talk about Robert," she started off, slowly. Her mom flinched when she heard his name, but Mwikali pressed on. "But I would really love to know a little more about him. About that side of my family. I think it's important that I understand where I come from. It's important to me."

Her mom held her gaze for a while before sighing and standing up. "Let me get something. Wait here."

Mom returned holding a photo in her hands. "I found this when we were unpacking. It was taken a few months after you were born, when Robert and I went to visit his mother and grandmother." She stretched out her hand. "You can have it. It's the only one I kept of him. Of us."

Mwikali's breath hitched as she lifted the photo and looked at her dad's face for the first time. All these years, she had wondered what he looked like, wondered if they looked the same, if she would recognize him if he walked by. And now here he was. Average height, clean shaven face, big smile.

The picture had been taken outside a building with

a sign that read "Tanus Restaurant." There were four people standing underneath the restaurant sign: Mom, Dad and two elderly women, one of whom was cradling a baby in her arms.

"Your susus — your grandmother and great grandmother — were so excited to meet you. They just kept passing you back and forth between them — wouldn't even eat their lunch. They didn't want to let you go," Mom said, smiling tearfully.

Both of the women had Mwikali's large almond eyes, and the older one had a dimpled smile, just like her dad. They all had the same rich, brown skin.

"He left the morning after this photo was taken." Mom's voice was soft, sad. "I wish I could tell you why but...I don't know. Someone told me he moved to South Africa, took up a graphic design job there. That's what he was — a graphic designer. Probably where you get your artsy genes from. He was always sketching something, just like you. Always had a sketchbook close by.

"Anyway, I reached out to your susus when he left — they lived in Machakos town where his people are from, but they didn't know where he was, either. Hadn't heard from him since the restaurant."

Mwikali shook her head in disbelief. "But he looks so happy! How could he just ghost you — ghost *us* — after this?"

Mom pulled her in close. "I wish I had answers, honey. But he never gave me any. And then when the opportunity with the airline came up, I packed us up and moved away."

They hugged each other for a minute longer before Mwikali dropped her hands. "Thanks for this," she said, glancing at the photo. "And for telling me what happened."

Not in the mood to watch TV anymore, Mwikali went up to her room and flopped onto her bed. She stroked the faces in the photo, thinking about how everything in her life had changed after it was taken.

What would it have been like growing up with a dad? In Kenya? Knowing about her Intasimi bloodline all along?

Something wet landed on her hand, and when Mwikali touched her cheek, she was surprised to find her face wet with tears. She let them flow freely, allowed herself to cry it out. To feel the loss of her dad and the family she had never gotten to know.

Through sniffles and sobs, she glued the photo to the inside cover of her sketchbook. She thought about her father, her susus, and all the people who had come before her.

Suddenly, she felt the urge to draw. To honor them. To honor her gift.

The feeling was stronger than it had ever been. It felt like a ball of energy had exploded inside her, flooding her body and mind with adrenaline.

Xirsi was right. Seeing her dad, learning about him and how much her susus had loved her — all of it had lit a fire within her. She felt more inspired than ever.

Mwikali traced the outline of a Mugumo tree and colored in its thick trunk and sturdy branches with her oil pastels. She was determined to get the textures of the leaves right, so she went over them with different shades again and again. This sacred tree was where Syokimau's story began. Where *her* story began. It needed to be perfect.

Her knuckles ached by the time she was done, but she hardly paid any attention to them. She was too preoccupied with her majestic Mugumo tree. Its branches and leaves stretched to the edges of the page, its trunk filling out at the bottom. It looked incredibly real. Unnaturally lifelike.

Mwikali brought the sketchbook up to her face, closer and closer, until her nose was smooshed against the page. It actually smelled earthy, and felt rough against her nose, too. As if... *As if...*

Her eyes flew open. The tip of her nose was touching a tree. An *actual* tree.

Mwikali jerked back and looked around, her heart hammering in her chest. She was no longer in her bedroom. No longer in her house. In fact, by the looks of things, she wasn't in Nairobi at all.

A dense and tangled jungle surrounded her. The lively sound of woodland creatures filled the air. Mwikali's bedroom had been warm under the glare of Nairobi's afternoon sun, but the weather here — wherever she was — was cool and misty. It was morning.

Mwikali's entire body tingled. Where was she? How had she gotten there? It felt as if she was somewhere she wasn't supposed to be. Like how it would feel to walk into a room and have everyone suddenly go quiet and stare at you...

She began to make her way through the trees, marveling at all the wild animals she passed along the way. A dazzle of magnificently striped zebras casually walked around her as they grazed. Further along, a herd of gazelles leaped swiftly away when they spotted her. And when she heard a loud trumpeting sound, she crouched down in the tall grass and watched as a family of elephants — the smallest of which was the size of a car — ambled through and away.

It was then that Mwikali heard the sound of children. The giggling and playful laughter drew her forward, past the thick of the trees, toward a clearing. As she inched closer to the open space, a group of girls came into view. They looked to be around the same age as Mwikali and were spread out on their backs, talking to each other as they stared up into the sky. All were dressed in brown animal skins and decked out in beaded jewellery from head to toe.

Could she have stumbled onto the scene of a traditional play? A re-enactment of some sort?

Mwikali crept closer still, wanting to get a better look at their faces. Maybe she would recognize them from school.

SNAP!

The sound of her foot crushing a twig pierced the tranquility of the forest and sent the girls shooting into upright positions.

Mwikali froze. She reached down to clench her clothes in her hands like she always did when nervous, and gasped when her fingers touched something else instead.

She looked down at her body. She was wearing animal skins, too! With layers of white beaded strings circling her neck and waist. She was dressed exactly like the girls in front of her.

Mwikali looked up to find one of them smiling and beckoning her over. The girl looked strangely familiar, and as Mwikali walked cautiously toward her, she noticed the girl's big almond-shaped eyes and dimpled cheeks. She had seen this exact face before, except on a much older woman. The girl looked exactly like...like... her great grandmother! The one in the photo!

Now she understood why she had been feeling like something was off, and why they were all dressed the way they were.

She wasn't in the wrong place. She was in the wrong *time*.

The ~~Future~~ Past

Mwikali had somehow traveled back to a time when her great grandmother was her age.

Mr. Lemayian had told her that this was possible — that good Seers could see into the past as well as the future — but Mwikali had never let herself believe that she was capable of it.

The girl — her great grandmother — pointed at bundles of sticks on the ground and then at Mwikali's head. She spoke in a language that Mwikali didn't understand, but it was easy enough to figure out what she was saying. The other girls were already doing it. Following their lead, Mwikali picked up the bundle of firewood, which is what she assumed it was, and placed it on her head.

It wasn't as heavy as she thought it would be. Plus, she had a thick crown of hair that acted as a cushion. Some of the girls had loose Afros like hers while others were completely bald. Her great grandmother's hair was braided into thin, short locs that spread out from the center of her scalp.

None of the girls seemed to mind the weights on their heads. In fact, they looked to be having a great time, taking turns speaking in animated voices as they walked. More than once, they even stopped to laugh so hard they clutched their sides. And although her mind was still spinning from the fact that she had time traveled, Mwikali found herself laughing along when they playfully poked her ribs.

Together, they followed a footpath that led them into a compound that was surrounded by a thorn bush fence. As they walked in, noisy gangs of little boys and girls ran up to them and tugged at their skirts cheekily before running back to hide behind their mothers.

Mwikali's gaze floated around the homestead, from the series of small earthen huts to the animal sheds, and then back to the center of the compound which was a hub of activity. There were women cooking over stone fires, others weaving baskets on the floor, while more of them tended to small babies.

She noticed that the kids her age were split into two groups: the boys, who were taking care of the animals, and the girls, who were bringing in firewood and water.

Mwikali followed her great grandmother closely as she walked through the compound and into one of the huts. There, she embraced a woman who patted her fondly on the head. A woman with eyes just like hers. It was her great, great grandmother!

Mwikali's jaw dropped. Was this really happening? Was she really standing in front of her great grandmother and her great, great grandmother? She almost laughed out loud in disbelief.

The two girls placed their firewood on the floor of the hut and sat down. There, Mwikali's great, great grandmother offered them a basket of fat, juicy mangoes to eat. These turned out to be the sweetest mangoes Mwikali had ever tasted. Their syrupy yellow juice dribbled down her arms as she ate, and she was more than happy to chase each drop with her tongue from her elbows back up to her wrists.

Every time she finished one mango, she was handed another, until — with an extra full tummy — she let out a long, contented sigh.

"Have you had your fill?" the woman asked, smiling amusedly.

"I'm stuffed like a pig," Mwikali said, before sitting up in surprise. She could understand her! She turned to look at her great grandmother, to see if she could understand the young girl too, but the girl was nowhere to be seen. It was just her and the woman — her great, great grandmother — inside the hut.

"Mutanu left some time ago," the woman explained. "She's my daughter but she doesn't have the gift. She doesn't need to hear this."

For the first time, she noticed that her great, great grandmother's lips were not syncing with her words. She was speaking another language, and yet Mwikali could hear English spoken in her mind. It was like watching a foreign language movie, but having the English voice-over actor talk from inside your head.

"You... You're my great, great grandmother," Mwikali stuttered.

"You can call me Susu."

"And I can understand you?" Mwikali said, stumped.

Susu laughed. "Of course. The same Intasimi blood that runs through my veins also runs in yours. My stories are your stories. My words — your words."

"You already know about me? About what I am?"

The woman nodded. "I'm a Seer, too. I had a vision of you some time ago. I knew how powerful you would be, and that you were coming. Now, here you are."

Susu pulled out a small black horn from one of her baskets. It had intricate designs etched into it and a leather strap going from one end to the other.

"This is a divining horn. We use it to look into the future. It's very powerful and should only be used by those who know how," she said, before raising the horn above her head and shaking it vigorously. Whatever was inside rattled loudly, causing Mwikali to jump.

Susu lowered the horn and took the leather stopper out of its mouth. Then, she flicked her wrist, sending several objects flying out and onto the ground. "What do you see?" she asked.

Mwikali squinted at the things strewn on the floor. There was a piece of mud, a ball of fur, and some other small objects that she couldn't quite make out.

"I see a bunch of random stuff," Mwikali said, confused.

Susu smiled. "You see more than you think you do. You have sight beyond sight. The only thing you can't see is how powerful you are."

Mwikali shook her head." I don't know what they mean..."

"Yes, you do. Trust yourself. Trust your gift," she said firmly.

Mwikali looked again at the objects on the floor. Slowly, dots started to connect in her mind. It was like she was starting to recognize the random pieces for what they really were. The answers were right there, on the fringes of her brain — she just needed to reach out and grab them. It felt like the split second before you finally figure out the answer to a riddle.

She stuck her finger into the soil and started to draw what she was seeing in her mind's eye. The images were coming in pieces, like a jigsaw puzzle that she could only solve by drawing.

"Good," Susu praised. "You have all the information you need to face what's coming. It's time for you to leave. And don't tell anyone about your visit here — not until you know who to trust. There is one among you who is not as he appears." She placed her hand over Mwikali's. "And when you go back, find Tanu. That's how you'll unmask the truth."

"What's that?" Mwikali asked, still staring at the soil, running her finger through it. She was so engrossed in figuring out the meaning behind the pieces that it took her a while to notice the silence in the room.

"What's a Tanu—," she started to say, raising her head. But Susu was gone. Everything that was there just a minute before was gone. She was back in her bedroom.

"You're already dressed? Nice!"

Mwikali jerked at the sound of her mom's voice. She looked around and then down at herself, expecting to see animal skins, but found that she was back in her regular clothes.

Mom wrinkled her brow. "Wait, are you still wearing

what you had on yesterday? And why do you look so confused?"

All Mwikali could do was stare. What had just happened?

"Anyway," Mom continued, shaking her head, "come down for breakfast. I've made sausages."

Breakfast? Why would she be having breakfast? *Unless...*

"Mom!" Mwikali called out, as her mom started to walk away. "Is it...morning?"

Her mom looked at her weirdly. "Ai? Of course it is. And if you don't hurry, we're gonna be late for church."

Mwikali waited for Mom to leave and then scrambled over to her phone and checked the date. It was the next day.

She had been stuck in her vision of the past for more than sixteen hours.

The ~~Mask~~ Mission

It took ages to convince her mom that she wasn't ill.
Mom kept placing the back of her hand on Mwikali's
forehead, convinced that she had some form of fever-
induced madness that would explain why she had slept
all afternoon the day before and right through the night,
even refusing to come down for dinner.

Apparently, when Auntie had tried to wake her up
to eat, Mwikali had mumbled something about being
stuffed like a pig.

While scrambling to shower and change into her
church clothes, Mwikali noticed multi-colored pastel
stains on her fingertips. The kind she got when she did a
series of drawings. Had she drawn something during her
vision?

There had been no time to investigate before church,
but afterwards, she hid away in her bedroom and rifled
through her sketchbook for any new additions.

There were three new drawings! At what point had
she drawn them? Was it when she was tracing her finger
through the soil in Susu's hut?

A shiver rippled through Mwikali as she took in the first image. It was of a mask, shaped like a snarling demon and colored in with red and black pastels. It had cracked lines all over it, making it look like a completed jigsaw puzzle. Something about the mask made her skin crawl. Something about it seemed evil.

She was only too happy to flip away from that page and onto the next. There, she found a drawing of a stately-looking and elaborately-decorated office. Richly colored traditional fabrics draped the chairs, and a variety of wooden carvings and traditional weaponry stood on proud display along the walls.

In the middle of it all was a large, heavy desk centered on top of a zebra-print rug. A shiny blue, old-timey dial-up phone sat on top of the desk, looking like a prop from a movie.

Black Panther, Mwikali mused. If this was a movie, it would be Black Panther, and *this* would be his office.

She eventually turned to the next page. The final drawing was by far the best and brought a huge smile to Mwikali's face.

Odwar, Soni, Xirsi and her were all in the picture. Mwikali was at the center, holding her sketchbook. Odwar was standing beside her, while shadow-Odwar flexed a bicep down below. Soni stood on Mwikali's right, holding a staff above her head. And Xirsi was sitting proudly on a tree behind them with a bird perched on his shoulder.

Mwikali's eyes grew shiny. They looked like real warriors — so brave, so powerful, so cool! And she looked like she fit right in with them.

She looked like she belonged.

*

"OH YEAH!" Soni exclaimed, bouncing up and down on her butt. "You did it! You're back on your A-game!"

She was holding Mwikali's sketchbook in her hands, smiling from ear to ear as she looked over the drawing of the four of them. The two girls were seated across from each other on the sports field, waiting for Xirsi and Odwar to show up so they could spend morning break together like they always did.

Soni's face was lit up like a Christmas tree. "And can I just say that I look *bawse*! Is that a dancing stick in my hand? So cool! I'm serving *major* superhero energy. Like Shuri, with a dash of Storm, and a sprinkling of Wonder Woman."

Mwikali beamed and sucked on the straw of her bubblegum-flavored milk box. "Thanks. We look fierce, right?"

Soni took a sip out of her own milk box — a coffee-flavored one. "Girl, we look like *warriors!*"

"Hey guys! Guess who bought everyone samosas?" Xirsi piped up, as he bounded toward them. He was jiggling a brown grease-stained bag in his hand.

"Not me!" he snorted, before pointing at Odwar who was walking beside him. "It was Odwar. But I'm the one who remembered to pack the lemon slices and napkins. So, you're welcome."

Xirsi cheerfully unpacked the savory meat-filled pastries and dished them out, adding a squeeze of lemon to each one. They were sizzling hot, which meant they had to wait for them to cool or else risk burning their tongues.

"Mwikali, show them your drawing," Soni pushed, excitement bouncing off her.

Mwikali smiled bashfully as she opened up her sketchbook and held it up so Odwar and Xirsi could see.

Their jaws instantly dropped.

"*Niiiiiiiice!*"

"Bro!"

They grabbed the sketchbook and held it between them.

"This. Is. Epic." Odwar said, grinning.

"Ooooh, now we definitely need a cool, superhero team name," Xirsi added. "And code words, too!"

Soni rolled her eyes. "Code words?"

Xirsi clapped in excitement. "Yeah! Code words! Like, if we need to bounce, the code word would be 'ndizi,' as in banana. Get it? Banana split?"

"That's probably the worst code word I've ever heard," Odwar said, laughing. "Let's leave the imaginative stuff to Mwikali. She's clearly the most creative member of our team."

Our team? A warm feeling blossomed in Mwikali's chest. They had said stuff like that in the past. But now, for the first time, Mwikali actually believed it. After having a vision and then breaking through her Seer's block, she finally felt like a member of the team. And she didn't even have to hide who she truly was. She could just be herself.

At some point, she would worry about what all the drawings meant. But right now, all that mattered to her was how happy she felt...and how hungry she was. Mwikali smiled brightly as she prepared to sink her teeth into her samosa.

Odwar stopped her hand midway through the air. "Careful! The caterer said they're really spicy today," he warned.

Mwikali smirked. She might have been raised outside of Kenya, but her taste buds were Kenyan to the core. "I love spicy," she bragged.

One bite was all it took to realize she had made a grave mistake. Her tongue caught fire immediately and the heat spread throughout her mouth, right down to her tonsils. Tears and snot started to pour out of her as she frantically tried to fan her flaming tongue.

Amid noisy laughter from her friends, she surrendered her samosas over to Odwar, who stuffed both of them into his mouth with an "I told you so" look on his face.

"Mwikali," Xirsi started, once they had all quieted down. "If everything you draw is a prediction, then does that mean that we're really going to become warriors? Like for *real*?"

Soni plucked grass idly off the ground. "Guys, being warriors actually means fighting baddies — monsters, ogres, and who knows what else. Are we really ready for that?"

"We've been training and getting better and better every week," Odwar said, confidently. "And remember what Mr. Lemayian said — to focus on the helping people part, not the fighting one."

"Also, we're a perfect age set of superkids, remember?

Our bond means we're even stronger when we stick together. So, we just have to stick together," Xirsi concluded.

Sticking together meant trusting one another. Not keeping secrets. At that moment, a wave of guilt hit Mwikali. She still hadn't told her friends about her vision of the past. Susu had said not to tell anyone until she trusted them.

She felt like she trusted Soni, Odwar and Xirsi, but then again, she had trusted her best friend in Chicago too, and look how that had turned out. It had only taken one day for Amanda to turn on her.

And anyway, time travel? Visions of the past? Would they even believe her if she told them? Better to be safe and not say anything at all. At least not yet. She could tell them about the other drawings though.

"I also drew these," she said, flipping to the other pages of the sketchbook.

Soni scrunched her face. "Do you have any idea what they mean? This one is scary." She pointed at the devilish mask.

"And this one — is it an office? I've never seen it before," Odwar said. "Xirsi? Your brain is filled with useless info. Do you know what any of these mean?"

Xirsi shook his head. "I don't. But Mr. Lemayian will.

And he's actually in school today. C'mon guys, chap chap. *Ndizi.*"

Within minutes, they were seated on a small gray sofa in a sparsely decorated office. The only interesting thing to look at in the drab room was the blue dial-up phone on the office desk which looked like the one in Mwikali's drawing.

Mr. Lemayian had his nose in the book *Weep Not, Child* by Ngũgĩ wa Thiong'o, a book she recognized from her mom's bookshelf. Mom was super proud of her Kenyan book collection and had been over the moon when Mwikali had bought her Barack Obama's latest book to add to it. Reading books by Kenyan authors made Mom feel more connected to her culture, her roots.

Eventually, Mr. Lemayian snapped his book shut and leaned back in his chair. "Hey, kids. Sema — what's up?"

Xirsi stuck a thumb out at Mwikali. "Mwikali's drawing again and she drew a bunch of stuff that none of us understand."

"One of them is totally awesome, though," Soni added, eyes twinkling. "You have to see it."

Mr. Lemayian's eyebrows shot up. "Mwikali? Is this true?"

Mwikali shuffled her feet, suddenly nervous at all the attention. "Yeah." She reached over and handed the sketchbook to Mr. Lemayian, pointing out which pages were newly drawn on.

He started working his way backwards from the last drawing, smiling when he saw the one of them as warriors. "Nice," he said, nodding in approval.

"Right?" Soni squealed.

Mr. Lemayian's smile faltered when he turned to the next page, and then faded completely when he got to the jigsaw mask. Mwikali could sense that something was wrong.

"I told Mwikali that if anyone could understand what these drawings meant, it would be you," Xirsi said.

But Mr. Lemayian wasn't listening. His face was frozen in fear, as if he had seen a ghost.

"Is there something wrong? With the drawing?" Mwikali asked, worry beginning to worm its way through her.

Mr. Lemayian dragged his eyes away from the image of the mask. "Yes," he breathed, standing up to pace the room.

The four looked at each other and then back at their mentor. He was mumbling and grabbing at the sides of his head. They had never seen him look so flustered.

"You remember what Mrs. Amdany said?" he eventually said out loud. "About something coming?

I know what it is. It's this. The mask. I thought I had more time to get you ready before you had to face anything like this, but…" His voice trailed away into inaudible mumbles again.

Odwar shook his head in frustration. "Before what? Mr. Lemayian, what are you talking about?"

He stood still and swallowed a deep breath. "That is the Forbidden Mask," he said, pointing at the open sketchbook. "It was supposed to have been destroyed hundreds of years ago — shattered into pieces. But from the looks of it, someone has put it back together."

"What is it? What's the Forbidden Mask?" Xirsi asked, as puzzled as the rest of them.

Mr. Lemayian slowly lowered himself back into his chair, snapped the sketchbook shut, and pushed it away, as if even the sight of the mask was too much for him.

They waited anxiously as he pinched the bridge of his nose and steadied himself. When he finally spoke, it was slow and deliberate.

"Traditional masks are supposed to honor our ancestors. But this one… This one was made from the wood of a felled Mugumo tree by a council of elders who feared they were losing their authority. They needed more power. So they hacked down a sacred tree and, through blood magic, created the Forbidden Mask — an object designed to channel the power of restless souls. Their plan was to use it to destroy their enemies."

He sighed. "It was bad enough that they pulled the spirits of the dead into the mask — that they used blood magic to do so — but something even worse happened during the ritual, something they didn't expect. Their dark magic caused a rip between our world and the underworld. And on that day, thousands of monsters crossed over."

Odwar gasped. "That's where all the shiqqs and ogres and everything else came from?"

Mr. Lemayian nodded. "That was the day they entered into this world. And when they did, they broke through in a wild and uncontrollable rage, tearing apart everything in their way, including the council members. Not a single elder survived their rampage. Not a single one got to wear the Forbidden Mask. And the monsters? Even more of them would have broken through if the mask hadn't been destroyed."

"How? And by whom?" Soni asked, her hands gripping the edge of the sofa.

Mr. Lemayian hesitated and a strange expression flickered across his face. "The ritual leader who created the mask for the elders and led them through the ceremony was a man who called himself the Red

Oloibon."

"Oloibon…" Mwikali had heard that word before. Suddenly, she remembered. "But you taught us that Oloibons were spiritual advisors! That every village had one who would guide the people, and sometimes even act as a Seer."

"Yes, but this man, this impostor — the Red Oloibon — was nothing but an evil sorcerer. He wasn't a true Oloibon. The council elders went to him because he was the only one who would agree to do something so abominable. Luckily, the village Oloibon — their real Oloibon — stepped in before any more damage could be done. He destroyed the Forbidden Mask, and the door between the worlds was sealed."

Mwikali looked down at the jigsaw-like drawing. "But now someone has put its pieces back together."

Mr. Lemayian's face darkened. "The next full moon will be a harvest moon. In the days of our forefathers, the harvest moon ushered in the harvesting season. People spent that first night gathering in the fields under the full moon's light. It was under a harvest moon that the Forbidden Mask was first created, and under it that the black magic inside it will be awakened.

"Not only will it grant its wearer unlimited power, but the doorway to the underworld will be torn open

once again. This is what Mrs. Amdany and the rest of
the monsters are getting ready for. They'll do everything
they can to protect the wearer of the Forbidden Mask
and make sure that the rest of their kind are freed from
the underworld. And once all those monsters are here,
there's nothing to stand in the way of them ruling the
world."

Soni shot up. "Did you just say that the Forbidden
Mask would be awakened on the next full moon?"

"But that's..." Odwar continued, also standing up.

"Tonight!" Xirsi finished, rising beside them.

Mr. Lemayian slowly lifted himself off his chair and
walked over to Mwikali, who remained seated with her
eyes glued to her sketchbook. Fear, shock, and confusion
coursed through her and she jolted when Mr. Lemayian
touched her shoulder.

"The Forbidden Mask must be destroyed before
tonight's harvest moon. Before night falls," he said, in a
firm voice. "And it will be up to you, Mwikali, to destroy
it."

The ~~Heroes~~ Zeros

Mwikali gulped. "*Me?*"

"*Her?*" Soni echoed, sticking an upturned hand dismissively at Mwikali.

"Yeah, no offence, Mwikali," Xirsi began, flashing her an apologetic look, "but she just got her power back! And now you expect her to save the world?"

Mwikali flinched. She had no idea that her friends still thought so little of her. She stole a glance at Odwar. He had always believed in her, always thought of her as extraordinary. But he was quiet. Much too quiet. The kind of quiet that said he agreed with the others but didn't want to hurt her feelings by saying so out loud.

"The Forbidden Mask is enchanted," Mr. Lemayian explained. "Besides the Red Oloibon who created it, only a Seer like Mwikali — one who can see things that are hidden from everyone else — will be able to find it."

"Wait," Odwar said, finally speaking up. "If nobody else can see the mask besides Mwikali, then the only person who could have put its pieces back together is…"

They all turned to her and a sudden chest ache forced

a gasp from her lips. So, this is what getting stabbed in the back felt like.

"I didn't put the Forbidden Mask back together," she said, softly.

Odwar looked shocked. "No, that's not what I meant. I—"

"Mwikali didn't do it," Mr. Lemayian confirmed. "It was the Red Oloibon."

"But... He would have to be immortal to still be alive after all this time," Xirsi said. "Is that... Is that possible?"

Mr. Lemayian's eyes glazed over for a moment as he stared out into the middle distance. "It's not *im*possible."

Even as she reeled from the shock of how little her friends trusted her, something else gnawed at Mwikali's mind. Something about Mr. Lemayian. There was something he wasn't telling them.

He continued to speak in a monotone, still immersed in his daydream. "Whoever put the Forbidden Mask back together needs Mwikali for the ritual — a powerful Seer to behold the mask and crown its new wearer. That's why this is happening now, when Mwikali has come into her power. Mrs. Amdany spread the word among the monsters about her having sight beyond sight, and now everyone knows that the ritual can happen because the Seer is here."

Mwikali dropped her face into her hands. "If I wasn't a super Seer, or whatever, none of this would be happening. And if I hadn't gotten my Seer's block, I could have drawn this earlier and given us more time to find the mask!"

Mr. Lemayian jerked up and shook himself out of his daze. "You are who you were meant to be. And what matters is that you've drawn it now. You've given us a fighting chance."

"But how?" Mwikali asked, lifting her head up. "How am I supposed to figure out where the mask is?"

"Keep drawing. Keep believing in yourself. Remember, on the day we met, how scared you were that you weren't cut out for this?" he asked, with the hint of a smile. "Look at you now. You know more about our culture than just about anybody. You're drawing things that haven't been seen in centuries! You're every bit the Seer I knew you would turn out to be. And more."

Mwikali smiled back weakly. "So... Just keep drawing?"

"Just keep drawing. And the rest of you — Mwikali can't do this alone. She'll need your help. All four of you have to do this together."

"And what happens if — no offence, Mwikali — what happens if evening comes and she hasn't come up with anything?" Odwar asked, piercing a fresh hole in Mwikali's chest.

"That won't happen," Mr. Lemayian answered, without hesitation. "The four of you won't let it happen."

Xirsi raised a brow. "The four of us? Aren't you going to help?"

Mr. Lemayian started gathering his things. "While the four of you try to find the Forbidden Mask, I'll be coming up with a plan to deal with the Red Oloibon, once and for all."

Mwikali watched him closely as he packed his bags. He believed in her and she didn't want to let him down. Still, as she observed the slight tremble in his fingers and the weird look on his face — was it dread? guilt? — she wondered if there was more to this story than he was letting on.

*

Mwikali stared quietly at her sketchbook as she waited for class to begin. The others were seated in the desks around her but she hadn't said a word to them since they'd left Mr. Lemayian's office. Their words — how they still thought of her as some weak, pathetic *noob* — still rang in her head.

She was also trying to ignore the pressure she felt carrying the fate of the world on her shoulders. What if nothing came to her when she tried to draw? What if her Seer's block came back and she couldn't find the Forbidden Mask?

Her head snapped up when she heard Mrs. Amdany's voice at the front of the classroom. This was the first time Mwikali had seen the teacher since the attack in the Lost and Found room. She had gone on sick leave immediately after the incident. But now it seemed that she was back, and acting as if nothing had happened. Mrs. Amdany barely even looked at her.

"Today, Babu has invited visitors from the Ministry of Education to join our lesson," she announced, casting a glance at the two men in baggy suits beside her. "Try to ignore them as much as possible as they walk around the class. They're just here to observe." The men nodded in response, before taking up positions at the back of the room.

Mwikali tried her best not to make eye contact with Mrs. Amdany. The last thing she wanted was her raging out into monster mode again.

"Something's not right," Soni whispered, suddenly. She tipped her head toward the back of class.

Mwikali followed her gaze to the Ministry official in

the far right corner. The man had his eyes fixed directly on her. Eyes that looked hungry. Evil.

Soni cleared her throat to get Mwikali's attention back and then tilted her head toward the opposite side of the class. The other official was glaring at Mwikali, too!

"Shiqqs," Soni whispered, frantically. "I can hear their hearts. They're loud, fast."

Fear shivered over Mwikali. She turned to Odwar, then to Xirsi. Their eyes were wide, bodies stiff. They sensed the shiqqs, too.

In a flash, both men crossed the room to get to Mwikali's desk, sandwiching her in between them.

"We know what you are," they snarled in unison.

Mwikali squeezed her eyes shut. *Don't look. Don't look. Don't look*, she commanded herself. Xirsi had told her not to let the monsters know that she could see their true forms. These would be the first monsters she had seen since the ogre cop several weeks before, and there was no way she was going to be able to fake not seeing their true faces. Her best option was not to look at them at all.

"Why won't you look at us, little girl?" they hissed, voices layered on top of each other. "We just want to show you who we really are. We have nothing to hide. Unlike your precious Mr. Lemayian."

Mwikali's eyes flew open. What did they just say? She

flicked her head up and immediately wished she hadn't.

The men were far more beastly than any other creature she had ever seen. They had tall, twisted horns that reached high into the air, and faces covered with dark fur. But it was their eyes that made Mwikali's heart double into a frantic beat. They were red, fiery balls, crackling and sizzling as they burned into her.

A panicked whimper escaped her throat. It was all Mwikali could do not to scream.

"You *are* the one!" they said, small, sharp teeth glinting behind their wicked smiles. "The Seer with sight beyond sight."

At that moment, a loud crash sounded from the far side of the class. A crow had just slammed itself into the classroom window. It was soon followed by another. And then another. A whole murder of crows had amassed outside the Grade Six Chui window, cawing loudly as they hurtled their black bodies into the glass.

Kids jumped out of their seats and ran to the windows, completely unaware of what was going on at the back of class. They couldn't hear anything besides the loud screaming of crows.

For the brief moment that the two shiqqs were distracted, Mwikali turned to Xirsi who was waving his hand up and down with a frightened expression on his face. His birds were out of control and there was nothing he could do to stop them.

The shiqqs shrugged and returned their attention to Mwikali. "The harvest moon is coming, and with it, the destruction of the barrier between the worlds. Our brothers and sisters will join us on this side, and there's nothing you can do about it."

They leaned into Mwikali's face, their foul breath searing her nostrils. "Don't you want to be on the winning team, little girl?"

Mwikali scrunched her shoulders and drew back as far as she could. Just then, a movement on the ground caught her eye. A shadow. Odwar's shadow!

The quick, darting movement of his shadow must have startled the birds because they began to caw even louder than before. A series of endless crashes sounded as they slammed faster and faster into the window.

On her left, Soni was thrusting her hand back and forth at the shiqqs, but nothing was happening. "There's too much noise," she said, in a strained voice. "I...can't... focus."

Her hand was producing small waves of energy but all they were doing was pushing Odwar's shadow away. Every time it would get close to the shiqqs, a sudden burst from Soni's hand would blast it away.

"Is that all your pathetic friends have got?" the shiqqs mocked. "They're more zeros than heroes, don't you think? You should really consider switching sides."

Blood drummed in Mwikali's ears. They were completely powerless against these shiqqs. And if they couldn't stand up to just two monsters, how were they going to face a whole army of them?

"Mwikali?"

Babu squinted at her from the front of class, where he was suddenly standing beside Mrs. Amdany. "Is everything okay over there?"

Mwikali nodded, not trusting herself to speak.

"Come to my office for a catch up after this, eh?" Babu said, with a look of concern.

Mwikali's eyes flitted upwards. The men's faces had switched back to normal, and just as quickly as they had surrounded her, they scattered, leaving to follow Babu out of the room. The birds dispersed along with them.

Mrs. Amdany shot a triumphant look at Mwikali just as the bell rang. Students immediately broke into curious whispers about the birds and the men. Mwikali's friends raced to gather around her as soon as the teacher had left the room.

"Are you okay?" Odwar asked, breathlessly.

Soni shook her head. "That was bad. *Really* bad."

"And we're the ones who're supposed to save the world? We're toast!" Xirsi moaned.

Odwar placed a hand on Mwikali's shoulder. "Hey, are you okay?"

Mwikali's thoughts were scurrying around in her head. One leading to another, multiple dots connecting at once.

She recalled Susu's words. *"There is one among you who is not as he appears."*

And then the shiqqs: *"We have nothing to hide. Unlike your precious Mr. Lemayian."*

Finally, the look on Mr. Lemayian's face as he stared at the mask drawing. A look that spoke of fear mixed with guilt, like a thief who'd been caught red-handed. Like he hadn't expected Mwikali to find out about the Forbidden Mask.

She sensed it right down to the pit of her stomach — that he was hiding something. And now she knew what his secret was.

Mwikali looked at her friends, her chest heaving with the shock of knowing.

"I know who the Red Oloibon is," she said, her voice strained with fear. "It's Mr. Lemayian."

The ~~Phone~~ Safe

They pulled back from Mwikali as if she had just told them she had the plague.

"Ex-*cuse* me?" Soni said, frowning.

Mwikali hesitated for a minute. It was one thing to solve the clues in her head, but explaining her theory? She wasn't prepared for that.

"I think Mr. Lemayian is the Red Oloibon," she repeated.

"Mwikali, what are you talking about?" Xirsi asked, his brow furrowed.

Odwar looked at her worriedly. "Are you feeling okay?"

"I'm fine," Mwikali snapped, starting to feel irritated. "Listen to me. The shiqqs told me that Mr. Lemayian is hiding something."

"And you believed them?" Soni scoffed.

"It's not just them!" Mwikali bit her bottom lip, remembering that she wasn't supposed to tell anyone about her trip to the past. "Someone else said the same thing to me."

"Who?" Odwar asked, crossing his arms.

Mwikali shifted in her seat. "I... I can't tell you."

"You're not making any sense," Xirsi said, shaking his head. "Why would Mr. Lemayian send us on a mission to destroy the Forbidden Mask if he's the Red Oloibon?"

Mwikali squirmed some more. "I... I don't kn—"

"Do you have any proof? Besides the word of a couple of monsters and some mystery person?" Odwar badgered.

"I have a gut feeling about it. I know he's hiding someth—" Mwikali started to say, her voice shaky.

"I can't *believe* you right now," Soni cut in. "Do you have any idea how long it took me — *us* — to trust Mr. Lemayian the way we do? And now you're trying to say that we were...what?...wrong to trust him? That he's evil? After all he's done for us? You're unbelievable." She turned around and stomped out of the classroom, Xirsi following close behind.

Odwar stood and stared.

For a second, Mwikali hoped that he would listen to her explanation. Hoped that, unlike the others, he would believe her. But then he started to shake his head and Mwikali's heart sank when she saw the disbelief and disappointment written all over his face.

With a deep sigh, Odwar turned and walked away from her, too.

"Guys, wait!" Mwikali choked out, tears welling up in her eyes. But they didn't stop. Didn't even slow down. They were done with her. Done with the weirdo. The *freak*.

She slumped onto her desk in the empty classroom and cried into her arms until a pool of hot tears pooled around her face. She thought she had finally found somewhere she belonged and friends to belong to. But nobody was quite like her. Even among kids who were different, she was still *too* different. She was never going to belong.

"Mwikali?"

A rough tap on her shoulder made her sit upright.

"Is everything okay?" Babu asked. He stood hunched over her desk, with one hand on his cane for support.

Mwikali opened her mouth to speak but ended up choking back sobs instead. The worst thing anyone could do when you were feeling sad was ask if you were okay. It was guaranteed to make you feel like crying even more.

Babu nudged her up from her desk. "Come on, let's go to my office. We never got to have our chat after your first week of school. We can do that now."

In minutes, Mwikali was seated in one of the two chairs on the other side of his desk. One hand hugged her sketchbook close while the other dabbed the last tears from her eyes.

"I'm fine. I just had a small argument with my fr—, with some kids," she explained.

Babu nodded, slowly. "I see. Can I ask what it was about?"

Mwikali shuffled her feet. "They don't believe me. Don't believe that what I'm telling them is the truth."

"Hmm," Babu said in response. He removed his glasses and used a cloth to wipe the smudges off their thick lenses. His wrinkly fingers moved stiffly, and it took a long time before he was satisfied enough to put the glasses back on.

When he finally looked up, he wore a curious expression on his face. "Are they really your friends if they don't believe in you?"

Mwikali's nose started stinging again and she swallowed the lump in her throat. "I guess not."

"Go where you're wanted. That's what I believe. Instead of forcing people to accept you, go to those who already appreciate you for who you are. You'll never grow — never know how strong you are — until you stop looking to other people for approval."

As Mwikali blew her nose, Babu opened his desk drawer and pulled out a large wooden board. It had rows of pits carved into it with small round stones sitting in some of them.

"This is one of the oldest board games in the world," he informed her. "It's called Bao — that's the Swahili word for wooden board. Bao has been played in our country for centuries." He picked up one of the stones and dropped it into a different pit. "It's a complex game of intelligence, believed to have been the prototype for other board games, like chess."

Babu leaned forward and spoke excitedly, his eyes twinkling through his thick glasses. "You see, each player owns half the board. And the aim of the game is to empty all the seeds — that's what we call the stones — from your opponent's inner row and leave them without any more moves they can make." He stopped and sighed when he saw the puzzled look on her face. "It's complicated. Takes years to learn, decades to master."

"It sounds cool, Babu," she said, wondering what Bao had to do with what she was going through.

He leaned back in his chair. "I was the Bao champion in my village. As a boy, when other kids were chasing goats and climbing trees, I sat in the village square and watched the elders play. I watched until I could predict exactly how the games would end. I was able to calculate each move, anticipate it ahead of time. And when they finally allowed me to play? I beat them all."

He looked up at Mwikali with a pained expression. "They didn't like that. Didn't like that I was better than them, smarter than them. And the cleverer I got, the more the elders tried to tarnish my name. They told everyone that I was using witchcraft to win. It was a lie, of course. The truth was that I was special, just like you are, Mwikali. Unfortunately, sometimes it's the special ones who have to be okay with not being accepted by everyone. Once I learned that, it didn't matter what anyone else said or thought about me. I just continued being me. Just continued winning."

Mwikali understood what he was saying, but it didn't make it any easier. Losing her friends — her team — made her chest physically ache.

"Now, no more tears," Babu ordered, clapping his hands together. "What's that in your hands?"

Mwikali pulled the sketchbook away from her and lifted it up for him to see. She was more than glad for the change of topic. "Oh, this? It's my sketchbook."

"You draw? That's wonderful. I hope you joined the Arts & Crafts club. First meeting should be this morning," he said, cheerfully. "Can I see?" He stretched out his hand and Mwikali handed over her book, a little unsure about showing it to him in the first place. What would he think about all of her strange drawings?

He turned the cover and smiled when he saw the photo stuck to the inside. "Ah, are you the baby here? You were so tiny!" he exclaimed, when Mwikali nodded. "I'm guessing these are your parents and... grandmothers?"

Mwikali nodded again. "Grandmother and great grandmother. My parents were taking me to meet them for the first time."

"Nice," Babu said, his white head bobbing. "It must have been a very special occasion. Tanu's is a good restaurant."

Mwikali froze. Tanu's? She yanked back her sketchbook and stared at the photo. For the first time, she noticed the small gap between the "u" and the "s" in the restaurant sign. She thought it said "Tanus Restaurant," but the apostrophe between the two letters must have been too faint to see. It was Tanu's Restaurant.

"...find Tanu. That's how you'll unmask the truth."

So much had happened that she had hardly given Susu's last words to her any thought. Could she have meant Tanu's Restaurant? Is that where she would find the truth about Mr. Lemayian?

"Where's Tanu's?" Mwikali asked, already scooping up her backpack.

Babu's forehead puckered. "Opposite Shujaa Mall."

Mwikali's heart leaped. She actually knew where that was! It was one of the buildings she recognized during her matatu ride with Xirsi and Soni!

She whirled around and sprinted toward the door. "Thanks, Babu!" she called out over her shoulder. "For the talk and everything!"

Mwikali headed straight for the school gate. She knew exactly what she needed to do. To unmask the truth, she needed to go to Tanu's Restaurant. There, she hoped to find proof that would convince her friends that Mr. Lemayian was the Red Oloibon. That she wasn't the crazy weirdo they thought she was.

And she needed to do it right now. The sooner she proved who Mr. Lemayian really was, the sooner they could find the Forbidden Mask. It was him who had it after all.

With club meetings scheduled for the rest of the morning, Mwikali was able to weave her way through the school corridors unnoticed. Streams of students flowed every which way, searching for their club meeting spots.

Mwikali looked like she was one of them, until she walked past the Grade Seven Simba class where the Arts & Craft club members were supposed to be meeting.

She kept going until she was crouching behind one of the school vans lined up along the driveway. There, she

watched and waited for the guard at the gate to leave his
post. The minute he did, she slipped through the gate
and dashed out to the main road.

Mwikali felt relieved to have completed the first part
of the plan, but only a little bit. Her heart pounded with
adrenaline as she neared the road. The next part was
the one she dreaded the most. It involved getting into a
matatu.

A layer of sweat formed on her face as she stuck her
hand out into the road, trying to look as confident as
Xirsi had done. Thankfully, traffic was slow in the late
morning and the matatu that stopped to pick her up was
mostly empty.

She climbed in easily and had her choice of seats.
"Shujaa Mall," she said to the conductor, handing him a
fifty shilling note and praying that it was enough to get
her there. She remained with another fifty in her wallet
— just enough to get her back to school, she hoped.
With all her lunch money going into this trip, she prayed
that it would be worth it. Relief washed over her when
the man not only accepted her money but returned ten
shillings back in change.

Shujaa Mall was much closer than she thought.
Within a few minutes, she was standing outside one of
its many gates, staring at the "Tanu's Restaurant" sign

across from it.

Her entire body twinged with nerves as she waited to cross the busy road. She had no idea what to expect or what she would do once she got inside the restaurant. All she knew was that this was the only way she was going to win her friends back, and save the world.

She had to will her rubbery legs forward when the break in traffic came, and even more so when she reached the restaurant's entrance.

Fears and doubts raced through her mind as she stepped inside. What if she didn't find any proof of Mr. Lemayian there? What if this was all just a big waste of time and Tanu was something else? What if this was all for nothing?

The restaurant was small and airy, with white tables and chairs neatly arranged in front of a green counter. It was completely empty.

Not knowing what else to do, Mwikali walked up to the counter and rang the bell. A pudgy, balding man with a dish towel draped over his shoulder immediately came shuffling in from the kitchen in the back.

"Hello!" he said, brightly. "Lunch service doesn't start until one, but you're welcome to wait if you want." He pointed to a table nearby.

Mwikali shook her head. "I didn't come for lunch. I'm

here for... Somebody told me... I was told to find Tanu. Someone sent me to—"

"Tanu? As in Mutanu?" The man asked, looking surprised. "This restaurant was named after the owner's mother — Mutanu, or Tanu for short."

Mwikali's heart skipped a beat. Her great grandmother's name was Mutanu! This was her grandmother's restaurant! Were they here? Would she finally get to meet them? What would she even say?

"I'd like to speak to her — or both of them — please. Could you let them know I'm here?" she asked, unable to hold back the nervous smile creeping onto her face.

The man's expression turned sad. "I'm so sorry, but they both died some years ago."

"They... What?" Mwikali felt like someone had just ripped a hole through her heart. The smiling women in the photo, her family — gone, before she ever had a chance to know them. "They're both dead?" she whispered, the pain in her chest making it hard to speak.

"Yes. Sorry to let you know. The new owners only kept the restaurant name because of how much everyone loved this place. How did you know them?" he asked, sliding over a box of napkins.

Mwikali blotted her cheeks. "They were my grandmother and great grandmother."

"Wait, are you Mwikali?" he asked, eyes suddenly sparkling.

She looked up. "Yeah. But how do you know my—"

"Wait here!" He zipped back through the door he had come out of earlier, returning a few seconds later with a bulky dial-up phone. It looked like the one in Mr. Lemayian's office except it was black with white ring dials.

"She always said you would come," the man said excitedly. "She told all of us who worked here that if a girl called Mwikali ever came asking questions, to give her this." He pointed at the phone.

Mwikali stared at it, confused. "A phone?"

He smiled, knowingly. "Not just a phone. It's actually a safe with an eight digit passcode. They used them back in the day to keep important stuff extra secure." Sticking his finger into one of the numbered holes, he turned the dial around until he hit a metal stop and then let go so that it circled back to its original position.

"The passcode needs to be eight numbers — usually a date — and when you dial in the correct ones, the safe should open. You'll see when you put them in. Go ahead."

Mwikali's widened eyes flicked up to him. "What do you mean go ahead? I have no idea what the passcode is!"

This time it was him who looked surprised. "Really? Your grandmother said you would know. Said it was a day that was important to all of you. A birthday maybe?"

"My birthday?" Mwikali wondered, and when he shrugged, she stuck her forefinger out and dialed in her birth date. But nothing happened.

"Ah!" he exclaimed, snapping his fingers. "I should have known that that wouldn't work. Older people don't care much for birthdays. So, maybe it's not a birthday. Maybe...an anniversary or something?"

Mwikali dialed in her parents' wedding anniversary. She had learned it on the day of the family tree drawing, before Mom had revealed her father's name.

That didn't work either.

The man shifted on his feet, narrowed his eyes at her. "You *are* Mwikali, right?"

Sadness and disappointment fought a bitter war in her belly. "I am! But... I didn't really know her. We only met once. Just the one time when I was..." She allowed her voice to trail away as a fresh idea took root in her mind.

The day she met her grandmothers for the first time. It was a date that was important to all of them, and she knew what it was because it was scribbled on the back of the photo stuck inside her sketchbook.

It was the only other date she could think of. It was her last shot.

Mwikali's veins thrummed with adrenaline as she dialed in the eight numbers that made up the special date: 04.30.2010. The year she was born.

She held her breath as the circular dial spun back into position for the final time, and only blew it out when she heard a clicking sound. The top part of the phone popped open, leaving a thin gap between it and the base at the bottom.

With quivering hands, she lifted the upper portion of the phone. A small wooden box was tucked inside its hollow base.

Mwikali's mind swam as she unclasped the leather strap holding the box's lid closed. What if this was the proof she needed? The answer to everything?

She opened the box.

The object inside was instantly recognizable. It was Susu's black divining horn.

The ~~Rescue~~ Rule

The ride back to school was a mindless blur of disappointment and confusion as Mwikali held on tight to the wooden box in her lap. Yes, the horn was an important part of her family's history and she was grateful to have it, but how was it supposed to help her prove that Mr. Lemayian was the Red Oloibon?

Almost half the day had gone and she felt no closer to uncovering the truth — no closer to saving the world — than she had before.

Her thoughts continued to trouble her as she hopped off the matatu and walked toward the school gate. It wasn't until Mwikali heard a rustling from behind her that she noticed the two men who had been following her.

By the time she had turned around, it was too late. Two large hands had already reached out to shove her to the floor. She fell backward and landed on top of her backpack with a thud, the wooden box scuttling to the ground beside her.

Nairobbery. That was Mwikali's only thought, as fear

flooded her being. Xirsi had warned her what would happen if she wasn't careful with her belongings. And now, because she had forgotten to put the wooden box safely in her backpack, it was about to be taken from her.

But the sound that came next told her that this wasn't just a case of Nairobbery. This was far worse.

"So, you're the one everyone's been talking about?" someone — *something* — growled.

When Mwikali sat up, she found two ogres staring back at her. They looked exactly like the policeman ogre except for their eyes which were red and glowing, just like the ones of the Ministry officials at school.

The monsters with red eyes seemed to be different from the others. They didn't bother to hide behind human faces, didn't have to be angry for their monstrous sides to show. They *wanted* to be seen.

"Do you really think you can stop us?" one of the ogres asked, spit flying out of his mouth. The other one grunted out a laugh and began to circle Mwikali.

She let out a scream and craned around for anybody who could help. But the footpath toward the school gate was completely deserted. She was all alone.

"You're just a little girl," he continued, menacingly. Then, he stretched out his hand. "Give it to us."

Mwikali instinctively pulled the wooden box to her

chest. "No," she said, her voice hoarse and trembling.

The silent ogre stopped circling and began to move in closer, but his friend put a hand on his shoulder, stopping him.

"We're not supposed to hurt you. But we will...if you don't give us what we want," he warned.

All of Mwikali's emotions suddenly surged inside her, exploding to the surface as frustration. "I said no!" she shouted, hugging the box even tighter.

The talking ogre lifted his hand off the silent one. "Then we'll do this the hard way," he growled. "Go and get it," he commanded his accomplice.

Mwikali watched in horror as the ogre licked his lips and moved towards her. Every part of her mind was screaming for her to hand the box over, to save herself. But her heart couldn't let it go. It was a part of her family's legacy. The only part she had left.

The ogre grabbed her foot, and with one easy movement, yanked her closer to him — so close that his bullring touched her forehead. A long string of drool stretched down from his mouth, forming a puddle of brown spittle on her skirt.

CAW! CAW! CAW!

Crows suddenly descended upon the ogres from the sky. They swooped in all at once, clawing and scratching their faces mercilessly.

Mwikali heard someone calling out her name and turned around to find Xirsi running toward her — hands raised — with Odwar and Soni right behind him. Her friends had come to rescue her!

She scrambled to her feet, but just as she was about to bolt, one of the ogres grabbed hold of her backpack. Mwikali pulled and struggled against him until he suddenly let go, allowing her to break free and into a sprint toward her friends.

She didn't stop until she was by their side, and only the rumble of an engine behind her made her turn back round. Both ogres were seated on the back of a motorcycle. One of them was holding something up, brandishing it high in the sky so that she could see.

Mwikali nearly forgot how to breathe when she realized what it was. Her sketchbook. That's what they had wanted all along! Not the divining horn — her sketchbook!

She pulled her backpack around to her front so she could confirm. Yup. The zipper was wide open. The ogre must have removed it when he pulled her back. That's why he had suddenly let her go — he had already gotten what they came for. Her sketchbook.

All Mwikali could do was stare as the men sped away.

She had lost the key to tapping into her power. How was she supposed to find the Forbidden Mask now?

"Do you have any idea what you've done?" Odwar asked, through clenched teeth.

"I— I didn't know they were after my sketchbook," Mwikali stammered. "I tried to get away, but—"

"That's not what he's talking about," Soni interrupted. "Do you have any idea what you've done by skipping school?"

Mwikali blinked. "By... What?"

Xirsi sighed loudly. "Babu has only one rule that he's super strict on: no leaving school premises without permission."

"Yeah. And he has a zero tolerance policy when it comes to that," Soni echoed. "Anyone who leaves school during school hours without permission is automatically suspended. No questions asked."

Mwikali's breath hitched. "But nobody saw me. I made sure of it!"

"Charo saw you!" Odwar exploded. "How do you think we knew you were gone? I heard him talking about it in the Prefects' Lounge! And he's already reported you to Babu."

"So, I'm going to be suspended from school?" Mwikali asked, numbness creeping into her body.

"Do you not see us standing here beside you?" Odwar gritted out, before stomping away toward the school gate.

Mwikali shook her head, totally confused.

"We left school to come and save you," Xirsi explained. "Which means we're getting suspended, too." He turned and followed Odwar.

"Why did you guys do that? You shouldn't have followed me!" Mwikali burst out, unable to bear the thought of her friends getting in trouble because of her.

"We knew you would get yourself into a fix," Soni humphed. "Odwar insisted that we come and help. Do you have any idea how strict his dad is? There's no telling what he'll do when he finds out."

Mwikali fought back tears as she trudged behind her friends. And when they arrived at the school gate, all her fears were confirmed. Charo's smug face greeted them at the school's entryway. To his left, Babu leaned on his cane with his mouth tightened into an angry straight line.

"It's all my fault!" Mwikali sputtered. "I didn't know about the rule and I'm the one who really broke it. Please don't punish my friends! They only came after me because I was in trouble. They were just trying to help me, to bring me back. Please, they didn't do anything wrong! I'm the one who should be in trouble. Not them."

Babu sighed. "You didn't know about my rule, so I'll forgive you. But only you, Mwikali. The rest of you knew the rule and broke it anyway. It doesn't matter why you did it. Odwar, Soni, Xirsi — the three of you are suspended from Savanna Academy, effective immediately. Go and wait for your letters outside my office."

"Babu, please! It's not their fau—" Mwikali cried out.

Babu faced her, his eyes burning with an anger she had never seen in him before. "GO TO CLASS!" he thundered.

She clamped her mouth shut and backed away, sneaking desperate glances at her friends as she did. They looked like their world had just been ripped from under them. And it was all her fault.

With shaky legs and a chest wracked with sobs, she staggered away. She had lost everything. Her sketchbook, her friends, her only photo of her family. And what was worse, there was no way to find the Forbidden Mask now. No way to save the world. She was out of options and almost out of time.

Distraught, she walked past her classroom and all the way to the sports field, finally slumping down into the grass once she was at its far edge. She realized that she was still holding onto the wooden box and opened it up. A dry smile cut across her face as she took the divining horn out. It was all she had to show from her trip to Tanu's. And she didn't even know how to use it!

At that moment, an unusually strong gust of wind whistled past her and continued on in the direction of the Mugumo Groves. In her hand, the contents inside the divining horn rattled. She tucked the horn into the waistline of her skirt and threw the wooden box into her backpack. Then, she found herself placing one foot in front of the other, headed toward the trees.

The Mugumo Groves were much more intimidating from up close. The tall, ancient trees towered into the sky like castles. *Haunted* castles. Xirsi's words came rushing back into her mind — about how spirits hovered around Mugumo trees, and killed those who were unworthy. Was she unworthy?

Her stomach clenched as she remembered how Xirsi's finger had glided across his neck. *Toast.*

She took a step back.

Right then, another blast of wind howled past her, disturbing the trees' heavy branches. They creaked and groaned, and the sound of rattling from the divining horn joined in the racket. But instead of scaring her away, this time, the sounds pulled her in, closer and closer. Until she had walked completely off the sports field and deep into the belly of the thick groves.

MWIKALI AND THE FORBIDDEN MASK

The ~~Misfit~~ Chosen

The groves were shadowy and eerily silent. Mwikali wrapped her hands around her body as she walked, peering up at the giant trees that surrounded her on every side.

They reached high into the sky, with canopies so thick they blocked out the sun. It was hard to see and, more than once, Mwikali stumbled over the gnarled roots of trees that dipped into and out of the earth.

Then she heard a voice. But it didn't sound like any voice she'd ever heard before. It was wet and gurgly, like underwater singing. It sounded exactly like she imagined a ghost would sound.

"*Mwikali...*"

There it was again! And this time, the divining horn rattled too, as if it were answering the call. She held it still. Why was her horn responding to a ghost?

Fear gripped Mwikali's throat. "Hello?" she choked out. "Is anybody out there?"

Nothing but the quiet hum of insects greeted her back. And something else. Was that water? Yes, she could definitely hear the sound of moving water.

Mwikali followed the trickling noise to a small, rocky stream. Something about the flow of water stood out to her. Something about it was odd. Then she saw it — the water was moving the wrong way! Instead of flowing from higher ground to lower ground, the water was flowing in the opposite direction. It was flowing backward!

She had heard about places like these, where the natural order of things was disturbed. Places with thin veils, where the spirit world was so close that you could sometimes hear those on the other side. Mr. Lemayian had explained that they were often used as sites for ceremonies that celebrated the ancestors. The closeness of two worlds — of the living and the dead — sometimes made weird things happen. Things like frogs falling from the sky and water running backwards.

A chill slithered down her spine at the thought of a frog landing on her head. Still, she inched a little closer to the stream. She needed to check if the person calling her was inside the water.

There was nothing in there but her reflection. The water was translucent and looked refreshing, much too inviting to resist, so she cupped her hands and brought up just enough to splash her face.

It smelled fresh enough to drink, too. But just as she brought a handful to her lips, she remembered something her uncle had taught her. It was the night of their housewarming party — about a week after they had arrived in Kenya — and Mwikali had watched her uncle pour some whiskey on the ground. He called it a "libation" and told her that he poured a libation every time he opened a bottle of something special, as a way to pay tribute to the ancestors.

Mwikali hesitated. It wasn't whiskey, but it would have to do. She tipped her hand and poured a stream of water onto the ground. "Libation," she said, softly.

"Thank you, my child."

Mwikali jerked up and slipped forward, just managing to get her hands back under her before she fell head-first into the stream. She scrambled to her feet and turned around, expecting to see a transparent, flying creature wrapped up in a bedsheet. But what she found was nothing at all like the ghost she had braced herself for.

A tall, bald woman stood mere inches away from her. She had skin that glistened like glitter and eyes that sparkled with joy. Shiny copper jewelry clung from her ears and circled her neck, wrists, and legs. Her arms were stretched out wide, inviting Mwikali to gaze upon her but not to be afraid.

"Welcome to the sacred groves, where all who are lost can be found," the woman said, smiling.

The ethereal glow from her skin bathed everything around her in a soft, bronze light. Mwikali couldn't help but think that every drawing of yellow-haired, pale-skinned angels she had ever seen had gotten it wrong. This? This was what angels really looked like.

It took her a moment to notice the small gourd dangling from the woman's animal skin skirt. And when she did, her eyes widened in recognition. She knew exactly who this was.

"It's you! You're Syokimau," she breathed.

Syokimau's smile widened. "Yes, and I've been waiting for you for a long time."

Mwikali gulped. "You know who I am?"

"Oh, I know a lot about you," she said, with a knowing smile. "I know that you feel like a failure and a misfit."

"I always mess everything up," Mwikali sniffed. "Even when I try to do the right thing, I end up sad and all alone."

Syokimau leaned in, her brown face more beautiful from up close than Mwikali could have imagined. She smelled fresh and earthy, like the sweetness left in the air after a rain shower.

"You are never alone," she said, her voice loud and powerful. "Tens of thousands of ancestors stand with you, beside you. Always."

Mwikali realized for the first time that Syokimau was using her native tongue, and yet she could understand what she was saying. No voice-over actor in her head or anything! She could understand the language — Kikamba — and maybe speak it, too?

"But you guys aren't here anymore. You're all gone," she said, testing out her theory. Yup, Mwikali was actually speaking Kikamba. Her susu's language. *Her* language. Somehow, the words were just forming in her mouth without her even having to try.

"We *are* here. Ancestors only truly die when you stop speaking their names. And for as long as my blood courses through your veins, I'll be with you and my Intasimi gift will be yours."

"But I've lost it," Mwikali cried. "My sketchbook is gone. I have nothing. No way to save the world!"

Syokimau squeezed her shoulders. "It's not your sketchbook that makes you powerful. It's your belief in yourself. You're stronger than you know. You're a warrior. And warriors never give up."

Just then, as if responding to her voice, fat drops of rain started to fall. Wait, not fall — they were doing the opposite! They were rising up to the sky from the ground. Droplets of rain were being pulled out of the earth and into the clouds. They were moving in the wrong direction, just like the stream water was. But even though jets of water were shooting up all around them, their bodies remained completely dry.

"How will I get my friends to believe me?" Mwikali asked, her voice almost drowned out by the sound of the rain.

"Stay true to who you are. Never doubt that you are worthy of this gift. You were chosen for it. Believe in yourself and then make them believe in you, too!"

As sheets of backward-rain blanketed the forest, Mwikali noticed that Syokimau was getting harder to see — blurry, like ink smudged on a page.

"Never forget who you are," she continued, her gurgly voice sounding distant and muffled. "And don't give up on your friends. You're stronger together. Together, you're not just Intasimi descendants, you're Intasimi Warriors."

Hope surged through Mwikali. She had to get her friends to believe her. She had to at least *try*. The world needed them, just like it needed her to believe in herself.

"Thank you," she said to Syokimau, as the rain washed the last trace of her smiling face away and then stopped the instant she had disappeared.

Mwikali didn't waste another minute. She sprinted out of the groves and straight to Babu's office.

"I know you guys are mad at me," she blurted out, as soon as she was standing in front of her friends. They were seated on the bench outside Babu's closed door, waiting for him to type out their letters of suspension.

"But, please, you have to believe me," she pleaded, before they had a chance to say anything. "Mr. Lemayian is hiding something. Give me a chance to show you that I wasn't wrong about that."

Soni rolled her eyes. "Look, we're already in trouble over here. No thanks to you."

Mwikali clasped her hands together at her chest. "I know, and I'm *so* sorry. But we still have to save the world! Please, just trust me. Come with me. Let me prove to you that what I'm saying is true. Please!"

Not one of them moved. In fact, it was only Soni who looked like she was even listening.

Then, out of nowhere, Odwar rose from the bench. "We have nothing left to lose," he shrugged.

Xirsi sighed as he stood. "Might as well make the last minutes we have at Savanna Academy interesting."

"Phew! Babu takes forever to type, and this was getting high key depressing," Soni said, jumping off the bench, as well. "So? Where are we going?"

Mwikali stuck her chin out boldly. "To Mr. Lemayian's office."

The idea had been tickling the corners of her mind ever since she left Tanu's Restaurant. The old-timey phone that the divining horn had been stored in looked just like the phone in Mwikali's drawing of the Black Panther office. And it was the same phone that was in Mr. Lemayian's real office. Something told her that those two offices were linked and that the key to figuring out how was in that old blue rotary phone.

A few hours earlier, she would have been too unsure of herself to say her idea out loud. But not anymore. She was never going to wimp out on being her true self for the sake of fitting in ever again. From now on, she would be brave enough to be herself.

"Follow me," she said, her voice brimming with confidence.

She was leading them to Mr. Lemayian's office, where they were going to find the Forbidden Mask and destroy it, once and for all.

The ~~Red~~ Oloibon

They moved silently through the empty corridors and were able to slip into Mr. Lemayian's office unnoticed. Like all the other offices in the school, the lock on his door had been removed after the country banned physical punishment.

In years past, teachers would whip students with rubber pipes and blackboard rulers behind locked doors. Thankfully, the government had banned such punishments, and schools had stopped allowing teachers to lock rooms while students were inside, just in case some of them forgot about the new law. Savanna Academy had gone a step further and taken out the door locks altogether.

Mwikali closed the door gently once all her friends were inside. "That's not an actual phone," she said, pointing at the blue phone on Mr. Lemayian's desk.

Ignoring their blank stares, she walked up to it. "We need to dial in an eight digit passcode. It's usually some sort of date."

Soni groaned. "Okay. But just any random date? This

is going to take forever to figure out."

"No, not just any date," Mwikali urged. "Try and think of a date that would be special to Mr. Lemayian."

"Well," Odwar said, tilting his head. "It's not going to be his birthday — last semester he specifically skipped school on the day the other teachers planned a birthday party for him. He hates birthdays."

Xirsi twitched. "Yeah, but what about a birthday that's not *his* birthday. What does Mr. Lemayian love more than anything?"

"Our motherland," Soni said, imitating Mr. Lemayian's deep voice.

Xirsi smiled excitedly. "Right! So try Kenya's birthday — the day we took the country back from the colonizers! Jamhuri Day!"

"12.12.1964," Odwar said, shuffling from foot to foot in anticipation. "That's the date we officially became a republic. Go ahead, dial it in."

Mwikali placed her forefinger in the hole with a number 1 on it, and turned her hand in a clockwise direction, all the way until she reached the metal stop. She did number 2 next, followed by the remaining numbers in the Jamhuri Day date.

A loud clicking sound pierced the air. But it didn't come from inside the phone, it came from across the room.

Soni immediately ran over to the sofa. She dropped to her knees and looked under it. "There's a door down here!" she shouted, a moment later.

Within seconds, they had pushed the chair aside to reveal a wooden trapdoor with a flight of stairs beneath it. The door had already popped open, thanks to the telephone code, and the opening was just wide enough for one person to fit through at a time.

Odwar didn't hesitate. "Let's do this," he said, hopping down the stairs and disappearing into darkness.

The narrow staircase led them into a room that Mwikali recognized immediately. It was the Black Panther office from her drawing!

"*Whooaaaa*," Xirsi marveled, staring at a collection of large wooden sculptures while Soni joined Odwar at a display case filled with spears, shields, and other ancient weapons.

Mwikali found herself standing next to the imposing hardwood desk at the center of the room. A number of framed photos were arranged in a row atop the otherwise clear desk. She lifted one of them up for a closer look.

"Um, guys, over here," she called out, her muscles tightening.

The others quickly gathered around her. The photo

she held was grainy, with a soft brown tint and a date written in the bottom right corner: Nov 15 1925. There was a group of men in the photo, all wearing animal skins and seated on small wooden stools. One of the men was instantly recognizable — long ruby red locs, strong jaw, bright white eyes. It was Mr. Lemayian, looking as young as he always did.

"What the..." Xirsi was holding up another frame, which he twisted around so the rest could see. A date was stamped on that one, too. It was from 1957 and, this time, Mr. Lemayian was dressed in a suit, surrounded by a different group of men. He looked exactly the same age in that photo, too!

And on and on it went. They found photos from 1925 all the way to the present, with Mr. Lemayian looking the same age back then as he had a few days before.

Odwar sank into one of the leather armchairs. "I... I can't believe it. It really *is* him," he mumbled.

"He's immortal. He's the Red Oloibon," Xirsi said, shaking his head.

Odwar sucked in a deep breath. "We owe you an apology, Mwikali. I'm sorry for not believing you."

"Yeah. Our bad, Mwikali," Xirsi said, with a sheepish grin.

Soni ran up and hugged her. "*Sooooo* sorry," she said,

squeezing Mwikali tight. "Props to you for standing by what you believed in. And for getting us to listen even when we didn't want to."

Mwikali felt a rush of warm relief. It felt good to have her friends back on her side. "It's okay. We just need to believe in each other from now on. We'll be stronger that way."

Odwar stood up and did a quick 360, just as the lunch bell sounded off. "It's one o'clock. We need to hurry up and find the Forbidden Mask so we can destroy it before tonight. It must be somewhere around here. Anyone have any ideas?"

Mwikali squinted at the ground. Something wasn't right. Her gut was telling her that the mask wasn't in that room. But just as she opened her mouth to say something to her friends, a loud voice interrupted her.

"WHAT ARE YOU KIDS DOING IN THERE?"

A screen had flickered to life on the wall behind the desk to display Mr. Lemayian's angry face. He must have had a security system.

Odwar stepped forward, with his hands clenched into fists. "We know who you are, Red Oloibon!" he grunted. "And we are going to destroy the Forbidden Mask."

Mr. Lemayian's face went blank, the fire quickly dying from his eyes. He looked around the room, from one face to the next, before his shoulders slumped. "Is that... Is that who you kids think I am? Is that why you're in there?"

Soni pointed at the photos on the desk. "Um...*duh?* We know you're immortal."

Mr. Lemayian nodded. "Oh, you've seen those." He rubbed the centre of his forehead tiredly. "Sit down. There's something I need to tell you."

Nobody moved.

"I'm not the Red Oloibon," he said, earnestly.

At her waist, Mwikali's horn rattled and a feeling of calm settled over her. Mr. Lemayian meant them no harm, she could sense it. "It's okay, guys," she said, taking a seat on a sofa covered in brightly-colored East African fabric. "Let's hear him out. I think he's telling the truth."

The others gawked at her with creased foreheads and knitted brows, but followed her lead. They chose to believe her, and together they sat side by side, staring expectantly at Mr. Lemayian.

He blew out a long breath. "I told you about the Red Oloibon — the evil sorcerer who created the Forbidden Mask. I also told you about the village Oloibon who destroyed it. I'm not the Red Oloibon. I'm the *other* Oloibon — the real one. A spiritual advisor. It was the elders of my village who went to the Red Oloibon to ask for help, and created the mask."

They looked at each other in shock and then back at him. So he continued.

"That was the worst day of my life. I've never forgiven myself for it. I should have stopped them from going to that wretched man. But I didn't think he would actually be able to do it! So, everything that happened to them was my fault. The fact that monsters roam this earth, that the mask was created... All of it. My fault."

"But how are you still alive? That was hundreds of years ago! Are all Oloibons immortal?" Xirsi probed, as stunned as the rest of them.

"No," Mr. Lemayian shrugged. "And the truth is, at first I didn't know why I stopped aging. I thought I was being punished for allowing the Forbidden Mask to come into existence — being forced to live with the consequences of my actions. But then, I met you kids." He looked at Odwar, Soni and then Xirsi.

"I knew how special you were. Your powers were already strong for your age, and they were amplified even more when you were together. I thought that maybe I was left here — made immortal — so that I could teach you how to nurture your gifts. I convinced myself that my true purpose was to be your guide. Your Oloibon."

He turned to Mwikali with shiny eyes and the hint of a smile. "But then, you came along and drew the Forbidden Mask. And that's when I knew why I'd been kept alive all these years. It was to wait for all four of you — the Intasimi Warriors. You're the only ones who can correct my mistake. By destroying the Forbidden Mask, once and for all."

"Your shame," Mwikali said, softly. "That's what you were hiding. That was your secret."

He sighed. "I'm sorry for keeping this from you. Sorry you had to find out like this. I promise not to keep any more secrets from you in the future."

"There won't be a future to speak of if we can't find the mask," Soni said, throwing her hands up in the air. "Now that we've ruled out Mr. Lemayian as the Red Oloibon, we're back to square one. And now half the day has gone!"

Mwikali jerked up. "Mr. Lemayian, you and the Red Oloibon are from the same time. I mean, don't you know what he looks like? Shouldn't you be able to pick him out?"

"Unfortunately, no," he answered, frowning. "The Red Oloibon always wore a ceremonial mask, always hid his face. Plus, he's a sorcerer. He could disguise himself to look any way he wanted."

Xirsi groaned, loudly. "So, he could be anyone. And with Mwikali's sketchbook gone, she has no way of finding out who he is or where he's keeping the mask!"

"Your sketchbook is gone?" Mr. Lemayian asked, his brows raised in surprise.

Mwikali nodded while reaching for her waist. Her divining horn was rattling and she had an idea. "I may not have my sketchbook, but I do have this." She held it out so everyone could see.

"Mwikali!" Mr. Lemayian cried out, in awe. "Where did you get that? It's... It's older than I am!"

She smiled and stroked the horn's curve. "My susu left it to me. I've never used it on my own before... But now, I'm willing to try."

"That horn is your Entasim," Mr. Lemayian said. "It's a bloodline heirloom that's meant to boost your power. If your susu wanted you to have it, it's because she knew you were capable of using it. But how did you lose your sketch—"

A power outage suddenly turned off the screen, together with all the lights in the room. Blackouts were a regular occurrence in Kenya, and rather than wait for the power to come back on, they groped their way out of the dark underground office and back up to the surface where there was more light.

Mwikali turned the horn over in her hands once they were up in Mr. Lemayian's regular office. She could feel the divining objects rolling around violently inside it, like they wanted to be set free. Like they had a message to deliver. A truth to tell.

"You've got this," Soni said, squeezing her shoulder. "We believe in you. Hashtag Girl Power."

Odwar and Xirsi nodded enthusiastically as Mwikali stood up and raised the horn over her head. She shook it cautiously at first, and then wildly, as waves of energy started to pulse through her.

Suddenly, she stopped and dropped a knee to the floor. There, she took out the leather stopper from the horn's mouth, and with a twist of her wrist, spilled the divining pieces onto the concrete floor.

To the regular eye, the contents of the horn looked both peculiar and random — a lump of tree bark, a hardened piece of mud shaped like a square, a tuft of animal fur, a rough copper coin. None of them would have made any sense to anyone, except Mwikali. To her, every item had a story to tell. Every object was part of a larger puzzle. Together, they unmasked the truth.

The words rushed from her mouth like the waters of a burst dam. "Tree bark from the sacred Mugumo tree, symbolizing a sacred altar. A sturdy piece of earth,

symbolizing a firm structure — one that's close by.
Fur from the back of a hare, the most clever of all the
animals. And a piece of shiny metal, shaped like the sun,
to symbolize time."

She gasped as the revelation found its way to her
mind and then her mouth. "The Forbidden Mask has
been hidden in a building close by — a sacred one — by
someone cunning. If we don't destroy it before the sun
goes down, we'll be too late."

The ~~Descendants~~ Warriors

There was only one sacred building they could think of that was nearby — the Savanna Chapel, a two hundred-year-old building built by colonizers in the early 19th century. The chapel was listed as a national historic site and sat idle on the far side of the school's parking lot for most of the week. School masses were held there every Friday, and on Sundays, a local church group used it for services.

With as much stealth as their speed allowed, they raced up the building's concrete steps and toward its entrance. The chapel's arched wooden doors creaked loudly as they pushed past them, disrupting the stillness that engulfed the empty building.

Mwikali's legs turned wobbly as she stepped inside the church. It looked ordinary enough, with pews lined up in front of an altar and colored rays of light filtering through stained glass windows. But there was something about the building that made her spine tingle.

"This place weirds me out," Odwar whispered, looking at his faint shadow on the floor. "The sooner we get out of here, the better."

"Do you guys hear that?" Soni asked suddenly, her head cocked.

After a small pause to listen, they shook their heads.

"A drum. A goat skin drum," Soni said, straining her ear toward a sound only she could hear. She moved her hands up and down like she was beating a drum. "Boom pata pata pata boom pata pata pata... You guys seriously don't hear that?"

"Nope," Xirsi replied. "But whatever you're hearing must be coming from over there." He pointed to a small, narrow door behind the altar. "Every living thing inside this chapel — every ant, fly, and roach — is avoiding that room."

Odwar was the first to start moving, his shadow already having taken off in that direction. "Yeah, that's definitely where we look first."

Mwikali tried to steady her nerves as they approached, but it was no use. Her body was cold with dread. Whatever was hidden behind that door was powerful beyond measure.

Odwar squeezed the door handle. "Locked," he reported. His shadow, faint as it was in the absence of full light, kept running back and forth between him and the door.

"Can your shadow get in?" Mwikali asked, curious.

Odwar shook his head. "It can't go anywhere I can't see." He tipped his face to the ceiling and sucked in a quick breath before ramming his shoulder into the door. Three hard collisions later, it burst open.

The room inside was large and completely bare — no furnishings, no paint on the walls. The only thing inside was a massive tower of greyish white rocks. They took up nearly all the space on the floor and reached up so high that they nearly touched the chapel's tall ceiling.

"*There*," Soni said, pointing at the rock structure. "That's where the drumming's coming from. From inside those rocks."

Odwar remained standing at the door with his eyes bulging out of their sockets. "Kit-Mikayi," he mumbled. "This is Kit-Mikayi. But, it doesn't make any sense... What's it doing here?"

Xirsi waved his hand in front of Odwar's face. "Haiya! Bro? Are you okay? What's Kit-Mikayi and why shouldn't it be here?"

"Kit-Mikayi is sacred... It's a sacred place," Odwar said, his eyes glazed. He blinked a couple of times and then started over. "Kit-Mikayi is an ancient rock formation that has been around since the beginning of time. Nobody knows who built it, or when, or even how.

It's always just been there. The thing is, Kit-Mikayi isn't supposed to be here. It's supposed to be 300 miles away near Kisumu, the town where my dad grew up."

He turned to look at the rocks again. "I've visited Kit-Mikayi a million times and I know this is it. You see the way the boulders are arranged? With some rocks stacked up on the right, some on the left, and others further in? This is exactly what Kit-Mikayi looks like. Exactly."

"Okay. *Super* weird that the giant rocks are here. Got it," Soni said, walking toward the center of the room. "But, what's the deal with them? What makes them so special?"

Odwar thought about it for a while. "Well, there are many different myths about Kit-Mikayi, but they all have a few things in common." He began to count off fingers as he talked. "One, they say it's sacred. Two, that there's something special hidden inside the rocks. And three, that anyone who goes around Kit-Mikayi seven times will die, and only if their heart is strong enough will they be reborn anew."

The tightness in Mwikali's chest suddenly loosened as a sense of knowing spread through her body. "We need to go around Kit-Mikayi seven times," she said.

"What?" Xirsi yelped. "Odwar literally just said that anyone who goes around it seven times will die."

"I know," Mwikali said, softly. "But he also said that those with strong hearts will be born anew. I believe our hearts are strong enough. I believe in us."

She could see the fear in their eyes and couldn't help but feel some of it start to seep into her bones, too. But then the words of her ancestors came rushing into her mind.

"*Trust yourself. You know more than you think you do.*"

"*Believe in yourself and then make them believe in you.*"

Mwikali looked at each of her friends' faces. "Over the past day and a half, I've had visions that have brought me face to face with my great great grandmother and Syokimau."

She waited for the gasps and exclamations of shock to die down before she continued. "They both told me the same thing. We're stronger than we know, because we're not just Intasimi descendants, we're Intasimi Warriors."

Mwikali raised her chin and straightened her back. "I know we can do this. Do you trust me?" she asked.

Odwar didn't hesitate. "I made the mistake of not trusting you before. I'm not going to do it again. Let's do this." He strode over to her side and gripped her hand in his.

"Intasimi Warriors for life," Xirsi quipped, pumping his hand in the air before joining them.

Soni groaned dramatically and then clasped hands with Xirsi, forming the final link in the chain. "Fine. But if we get reborn as goats, I'm going to kill you guys."

All four, hands joined, began to circle Kit-Mikayi. The first four rotations felt normal. They started to feel tired during the fifth. By the time they were midway through the sixth, their legs felt like lead.

When they completed their seventh walk around the sacred rocks, everything went black. They succumbed to the darkness.

*

Mwikali's eyes fluttered open to the sound of drums and singing.

For a moment, she remained still, lying flat on her back listening to the steady rhythm of beats and throaty chants that filled the room. The sound was mesmerizing enough to keep her lulled in a daze for several minutes, before fragments of memories broke their way through to her mind. The Forbidden Mask... Kit-Mikayi... Her and her friends going around the rocks... Wait, her friends! *Where were they?*

She sat up and immediately doubled over coughing. The air was filled with dust, the floor covered in rubble.

Kit-Mikayi had collapsed!

Mwikali searched frantically for the others and felt her heart drop when she saw them across the room, sprawled on the floor with their eyes closed, motionless.

Anyone who goes around the rocks seven times will die...

Odwar's words haunted her as she scrambled to her feet. "Guys!" she screamed, terror thundering down on her. "Guys, wake up!"

But it was no use, the endless chanting and loud thumps from the drums were louder than she was, and even they weren't enough to wake her friends.

Mwikali looked toward the center of the room, where the music seemed to be coming from. She gasped. The deafening sounds were emanating from a single object that hovered in the air. It was in the same spot that Kit-Mikayi had once stood. It must have been hidden inside it all along.

She recognized the scowling, devil face immediately. It was the Forbidden Mask. They had found it!

"We did it, we found the Forbidden Mask!" Mwikali shouted.

As soon as she said its name, all the music suddenly stopped and the room fell deadly silent. The chapel itself seemed to be holding its breath.

Then, an evil laugh rang loud and hollow through

the building, followed by footsteps, growing louder and louder as the owner of the laugh walked down the chapel aisle.

Tap. Tap. Tap.

Mwikali stared helplessly at the door. She had no doubt that the figure who would appear in front of her next would be the Red Oloibon. This is where he had been keeping the Forbidden Mask, waiting until the full moon to use it.

Tap. Tap. Tap.

The footsteps were edging closer. The Red Oloibon would be inside the room any minute now, and there was nowhere for her to hide. No way for her to wake her friends so they could hide.

Tap. Tap. Tap.

There was something familiar about that walk. She had heard it several times before. Only one person made that sound when he walked. *But it couldn't be...* There was no way the Red Oloibon was—

"Babu?"

An evil smile sliced across the old man's face as he appeared at the door.

"Hello, Mwikali. You're finally here."

The ~~Grandpa~~ Supervillain

The smug look on Babu's face made Mwikali feel sick. He had deceived them all with his sweet grandpa act, all to cover up the fact that he was the cunning and clever hare. He was the Red Oloibon.

She had been too blinded by his wrinkly smile to see it before. But now, she remembered the quick tapping sounds she had heard behind her, right before she was shoved into the Lost and Found closet with Mrs. Amdany. Babu. He's the one who had pushed her in there.

And those shiqqs from the Ministry who had surrounded her desk? They had come to the school upon Babu's request. He had invited them — invited shiqqs — into Mwikali's class.

The ogres waiting for her outside of school after her visit to Tanu's? She had mentioned the restaurant to Babu before she left his office. He must have suspected where she was going and arranged for the ogres to attack her when she returned.

Anger flared inside her. She was not going to let him

win. And there was no time to think twice about it.

Mwikali took two running strides forward, leaped onto one boulder and then onto a larger one beside it, before springing up to snatch the Forbidden Mask out of the air.

She expected Babu to be surprised, angry even, that she had grabbed the mask, but his triumphant expression remained unchanged. He barely seemed to notice what she had done.

Meanwhile, Mwikali had started to feel strange as soon she had the mask in her hands. The enchanting music had started back up again with the chants now sounding out her name — *"Mwikali! Mwikali!"* — over and over again.

The calls were coming from the Forbidden Mask. It was calling out to her. Praising her. Making her feel wanted, adored, powerful.

Babu jutted out his bottom lip in the direction of her friends. "I was trying to get rid of them earlier with the suspension. But it looks like the mask did that for me."

Fear twisted inside Mwikali's stomach as she glanced at her friends' still bodies. "What's wrong with them? Will they be okay?"

"Only the strong of heart are born anew. I guess your useless friends didn't make the cut."

Terror sealed Mwikali's throat. *No.* It couldn't be. Her friends were going to be okay. *They had to be.*

"Forget about them. They're nothing like you, Mwikali," Babu said, eyes flashing wildly. "You're ten times more special than they could ever be. I told you before, you and I are the same. We were born to stand out. Born to rule."

"I am *nothing* like you!" Mwikali fired back. "You're the Red Oloibon. You're evil!"

Babu's eyebrows shot up in surprise. "You know my name? Well then, there's no need for pretenses."

He tossed his cane and glasses aside, then straightened his back from hunched into a perfectly upright position. Mwikali's stomach lurched as she watched all the creases and moles clear from his face, leaving behind smooth, taut skin.

It had all been an elaborate disguise, right down to the wrinkly smile he had used to win her over. Babu, the sweet grandpa, didn't actually exist.

"You're... You're not—" She struggled to get her words out through the shock.

"Old?" Babu offered. "Oh, I'm very old. Ancient, in fact. But I can look as old or as young as I please. I chose old. Young people attract too much attention, you see, and I needed to stay hidden. I needed a mask to hide

199

behind, as it were. Pretending to be an old man was the perfect disguise. Your generation thinks nothing of its elders. You don't see them at all. And so, I pretended to be Babu as I waited...for you."

"You need me for the ritual," Mwikali said, through clenched teeth.

"Exactly. The Forbidden Mask ritual only has one requirement — that he who wears the mask must be enthroned by another who can behold the mask. I've waited for centuries to find an Intasimi with just the right power. And you, a Seer with sight beyond sight, are the perfect one! I've chosen you to rule the world beside me."

"No," Mwikali breathed. "I would never!"

Like a hyena circling its prey, Babu smirked as he walked tight circles around Mwikali. "Yes, you will. You know why? Because people like us will always be shunned by those whose brains are too small to comprehend our greatness. Like the elders did to me, like your friends did to you. Wouldn't you want to live in a world where we don't have to hide how special we are? Where we don't have to dilute ourselves for anyone? That's the kind of world we'll create!"

Mwikali shook her head fervently. "But... The monsters! The Forbidden Mask will destroy the veil and let all the monsters in!"

"We would rule over them!" Babu boomed, his voice so deep that it shook the very ground they were standing on. "The mask would give us the power to make the monsters our underlings. Think of how unstoppable we would be with a whole army of monsters at our command!"

Mwikali tightened her fists around the mask, loud chants of her name still blaring in her ears. She allowed herself to imagine what it would be like to have millions of shiqqs and ogres bowing to her and calling out her name instead of attacking her and making her tremble with fear. She imagined what it would be like to never be made to feel like a freak.

"You could feel like this forever if you wanted. Strong, like nobody could ever hurt you again," Babu pressed, eyes darting from Mwikali to the mask. "You know, when I was younger, the elders and the other Oloibons made me feel like I could never be one of them. Until I realized that I didn't *want* to be one of them. I wanted to be much, much more. That's when I christened myself the Red Oloibon and vowed to show them — to show everyone — how great I could be. And now, with the mask, the two of us could be the greatest beings to ever exist!"

Mwikali felt her arms lifting the Forbidden Mask up to his face, ready to crown him. It was like being in that weird state between wakefulness and sleep. The one where you trip over imaginary steps and have thoughts that don't make sense. Where you don't have full control over your body, but still have a chance to decide if you want to wake up or give in to the numbing darkness of sleep.

Babu lowered his face towards her hands, towards the mask, eyes gleaming with anticipation.

"Mwikali! Don't listen to him!"

Odwar's voice sounded hoarse but forceful enough to jolt Mwikali awake. A wave of relief washed over her as she turned to find all three of her friends sitting up.

"Did we find the Forbidden Mask?" Soni mumbled, rubbing her eyes.

Mwikali pumped the mask up in the air, but got no reaction out of her friends. "You guys can't see it?"

Xirsi shook his head. "Nope, but if that's what's in your hand, you have to destroy it. Do it now, Mwikali. Destroy the mask!"

She stared at the mask's curved edges. It was much more powerful than she had thought it would be. It's power was enticing. Hypnotic. She found herself wanting to cradle the mask in her arms rather than destroy it.

"You're going to listen to them?" Babu hissed. "These so-called friends? The ones who never believed in you in the first place? You'll always be an outcast. A misfit. And unless you take the power that's inside that mask, you will always be weak and alone."

Mwikali's head snapped up. Syokimau's words ricocheted around her mind, breaking the Forbidden Mask's spell over her. The divining horn rattled as the truth cloaked her.

"I am never alone," she said, her voice loud and strong. "Tens of thousands of ancestors stand with me, beside me. Always."

She raised the Forbidden Mask high above her head. "And true power doesn't come from material things — not a sketchbook, not a mask. True power comes from believing in yourself!"

As she said these last words, she brought the mask crashing down to the ground, where it shattered into tiny pieces.

Tears of relief flooded Mwikali's eyes as she slumped to the floor. It was over. The mask was destroyed. The world — saved.

Her friends cheered as they surrounded her with hugs, and if it wasn't for the grating sound of Babu's dry cackle, they might have continued celebrating.

His mocking laugh made Mwikali pause, turn to the space on the floor where the splinters of the Forbidden Mask used to be. They were no longer there.

Instead, every broken piece was floating in the air. And then, one by one, the wooden chips began to attach themselves to each other, until the entire mask was whole once more.

"Did you think it would be that easy?" Babu bellowed. "The Forbidden Mask is indestructible! Every single fragment holds a thousand trapped spirits. They have nowhere else to go except back to each other. And they will never allow themselves to be destroyed. Ever."

The ~~Goats~~
G.O.A.Ts

"So, it's you. It's been you all this time," Mr. Lemayian said, suddenly appearing in the doorway. Mwikali didn't know how long he had been there, but it was clearly long enough to know that Babu was the Red Oloibon.

Babu snickered. "You've always been blind Lemayian! Even back then, you never understood how powerful the mask was. You actually thought it was destroyed when you left it in pieces."

"And you let me think I had succeeded, just so you could buy yourself time," Mr. Lemayian realized.

"Once it was created, all I needed was to keep it secure, so I re-created Kit-Mikayi, the fortress of stone, to keep it in. Then I waited for someone like Mwikali — a uniquely gifted Seer — to come along," Babu confirmed, smugly. "The council of elders deserved to be punished after what they did, after how they treated me. So, I agreed to help them, hiding behind my ceremonial attire so they wouldn't know it was me. I needed their blood to complete the ritual and, as soon as I had it, I let the monsters have their way with them."

"You knew the ritual would tear the veil — let in the monsters — and you did it anyway?" Mwikali spat out, disgusted.

Babu waved his hand, dismissively. "Monsters are easy to control, once you offer them a taste of the power they crave. I created a small army of them — red-eyed and thirsty for blood. But I'll need many more if I'm to create a better world."

"A better world?" Mr. Lemayian scoffed. "What kind of a world will it be if it's created from death and destruction?"

"The world is already filled with death and destruction!" Babu yelled, his voice filled with rage. "You think children can make it any better? I stopped believing that years ago, when my own children abandoned me, left their motherland for foreign soil. And when this greedy government began cutting down trees and kicking us out of our villages in the forest, did they come back to help? No. I lost everyone. Everything! And I realized that children are not the answer — they're the problem. All they do is consume entertainment and disrespect their heritage every chance they get. They're the reason our culture is fading away.

"You've been around as long as I have, Lemayian. You know that I speak the truth. We went from being a people that valued tradition to being a people without one. Kids nowadays — they hardly speak our native tongues. They seek information from the internet instead of their elders. They don't know a thing about our customs and ceremonies. They're not worthy of the Intasimi blood they've been blessed with. They can't bring about the change this world needs."

Mr. Lemayian took a step into the room. "There's much more to them than that. Powers awaken in the young because their minds are open to learning, to being taught, to change! They make mistakes, but they want to do the right thing. Want to use their gifts to serve. Unlike the old, they're full of optimism, of hope!"

"Hope?" Babu scoffed. "Hope will doom this world."

"No," Mr. Lemayian said. "Hope will save it." He looked behind him and beckoned to someone standing just outside the room.

Mwikali's mouth dropped open as she watched her mom step in beside Mr. Lemayian, followed by a bunch of other adults who she soon realized were her friends' parents. One of the men, the one standing closest to Mom, had dimples in his cheeks and almond-shaped eyes.

"Mom? What's going on?" Mwikali asked, shifting her eyes from her mom to the man beside her — her *dad*.

The sight of him made her eyes grow moist and she had to bunch up her skirt in her hands to keep her fingers from trembling.

It was he who answered her question. "Mr. Lemayian sought each of us out, told us we needed to form a council — like how it was in the old days. A council of elders to bless the warriors and punish those who stood against them."

His eyes softened for a moment, the corner of his mouth lifting into a half smile. "Hi, Mwikali."

Tears and love flooded her throat. She couldn't believe he was actually there, standing right in front of her. The father she had never met. "Hi." She paused. "Dad."

She wanted to run up and hug him, but the question in her head — a question she had carried around her whole life — held her back. Why had he left them? What reason could he possibly have had to abandon his family?

"This is the new council of elders," Mr. Lemayian announced, interrupting their reunion. "And I am their Oloibon. Warriors, you can leave us now. The trial and punishment of the Red Oloibon is about to begin."

"Mr. Lemayian..." Odwar said, hesitating.

"We'll be fine," he assured them. "We'll deal with the Red Oloibon once and for all. Right now, you guys need to take the Forbidden Mask and destroy it. Mwikali will show you how. May the ancestors guide you."

For the second time that day, Mwikali snatched the mask out of the air. She barely noticed the music coming from it this time. She was focused on something else. Something more important. Mr. Lemayian had dropped a clue in his words. *May the ancestors guide you.* He had told her exactly what she needed to do.

After exchanging quick hugs with their parents, the four young warriors took off running. They were shocked to discover that the sun was already red-orange and sitting low in the west.

"It's fifteen minutes to six!" Xirsi shouted, glancing at his watch in alarm. "We were in the chapel for hours!"

"At least we survived and didn't get turned into goats!" Soni reminded him.

Mwikali started running again. "We need to go to the Mugumo Groves! Now!"

Tension filled the air between them as they sprinted, each stealing glances at the darkening sky.

Odwar, by far the fastest in the group, was first to arrive at the sports field that led to the groves. "Oh no," he panted, pointing to the middle of the field.

"What— " Mwikali's words died in her throat as she followed Odwar's panicked gaze down the field.

An unruly line-up of monsters stood about halfway

in, forming a barrier between them and the groves. There were shiqqs, ogres and about a dozen other horrific creatures that Mwikali had never seen before. Every beastly face and fiery, red eye was locked on them, ready to fight.

"Are those what I think they are?" Xirsi asked, his face slick with sweat.

Mwikali nodded, partly distracted by the loud rattling of the horn at her side. "Monsters. A whole bunch of them."

Odwar dropped his eyes to the ground. "Kit-Mikayi changed us. We've been born anew. Look," he said, pointing at his feet. At that moment, his shadow lifted itself off the ground and began to whirl around him like a tornado of black smoke.

"I feel different, too," Soni said, clenching and unclenching her hands. "Stronger."

"Same here," Xirsi echoed, looking up to the sky.

"Guys," Mwikali said, looking worriedly from the sun to the field. "How are we going to get past them?"

Odwar stepped out in front of her, his shadow churning and raging around him like a beast untamed. "Leave that to us."

Soni took up position on Mwikali's right, with her hands raised, poised to strike. "Yup. We've got you."

"Wait." Xirsi closed his eyes briefly and the next minute, the sound of screeching and whooping broke through the air. A troop of monkeys with black fur and white throats loped across the field, while hundreds of crows flew in after them.

Xirsi and his animal gang took up the spaces on her left and back. "Now, we're ready."

"And, guys?" Soni said, as they prepared to move across the field. "This time, we work together."

With Mwikali surrounded, and the Forbidden Mask tucked safely under her arm, they stepped onto the field. The monsters took that as their cue to attack and did so from every direction.

Like a wind storm, Odwar's shadow whooshed ahead, cutting a wide path in front of them as monsters scrambled to get out of its way. The few who were unlucky enough to get trapped in the black cloud were completely blinded and groped around uselessly inside it.

Soni unleashed shockwaves through her hands that blasted the beasts backward with such force that it was almost as if she was shooting grenades out of her palms. She did it all without her earplugs, too!

The shrieking of Xirsi's animals was deafening. With bared teeth and razor-sharp claws, they bit, slapped, and scratched all who got near them. They even spread out across the field, taking the fight to the monsters by leaping onto their shoulders and pecking at their eyes.

Working as a team, the four of them were able to make their way down the field, but not nearly as fast as they needed to. With only a sliver of sun left above the horizon, there was still more than a third of the ground left to cover.

"Cover me!" Mwikali yelled, above the din of the battle. "I'm going to make a run for it!"

She bolted off, sprinting like a rugby player headed for the try-zone, bobbing and weaving her way past the monsters. As she did so, she realized that she was able to accurately predict every movement the monsters were about to make. She could tell ahead of time which side they were going to move to, so that all she had to do was go the opposite way. Kit-Mikayi had definitely changed them.

She was able to cross the last patch of field and, finally, when the finish line of trees was within reach, she dove and forward somersaulted into the groves — a place she knew the monsters were not worthy enough to enter.

The sun was almost completely gone — the harvest moon, moments from rising. All Mwikali could do was pray that her plan worked.

The sounds from the Forbidden Mask were louder than ever now. For the second time, she raised the mask above her head and, in that moment, it hit her: the voices were calling out not in praise but for help. All those spirits were crying out to her, begging her to set them free so that they could finally be at peace.

And that was exactly what she was going to do.

Mwikali thrust her hands forward, hurling the mask into the nearest tree.

It broke apart, just like she knew it would, but this time, it didn't put itself back together. Instead, its jagged pieces floated up gently into the air and then toward the Mugumo trees.

Traditional drums pounded out a steady rhythm. It sounded nothing like the music from earlier. The music from before was haunting and bewitching. This music was cheerful, filled with rich and beautiful singing. It made Mwikali twist her waist, stomp her feet and throw her head back with joy.

Happy tears filled her eyes as she watched each piece of the mask fuse with the bark of a tree and disappear. After hundreds of years, the trapped spirits were finally at peace in the sacred Mugumo tree forest — the earthly dwelling place of the dead — where all who are lost can be found.

The ~~End~~ Beginning

Mwikali fluffed out her Afro and gave herself a final once over in the mirror.

"Quit fussing. You look great," Soni said, as she washed her hands in the neighboring sink.

Mwikali just couldn't stop running her hands through her hair, and staring in awe at her own reflection. She looked so different!

After destroying the Forbidden Mask, she had walked out of the groves to find her friends waiting for her at the edge of the field. They had explained how the monsters had suddenly taken off running when they heard the beautiful music coming out the woods. Somehow, they had known it was over — that the mask had been destroyed.

With O-shaped mouths, her friends had stumbled over their words to ask her what had happened to her hair. Confused, it was not until Soni had handed her a small mirror that she had seen what they were talking about. Her black as night Afro suddenly had bright red highlights running through it.

She had been stunned. And although she had no idea what had turned her hair red, she had fallen in love with it immediately.

The adults had caught up with them on the field soon after. Mom had dashed up and wrapped her in a hug. "We're so glad you're okay!" she had said, her voice shaky with relief. "I'm so proud of you."

Mr. Lemayian had then explained how their parents had been his plan to deal with the Red Oloibon all along. That's where he had hurried off to that morning. He had contacted each of them, explaining that they had to meet with him to discuss a matter of life and death concerning their children. His lifelong research into the bloodlines meant that he knew exactly where to find each of them, including Mwikali's dad.

So, while Mwikali had been sneaking out of school, getting attacked by monsters for the second time that day, and talking to Syokimau in the sacred groves, her mom, dad and the rest of the parents had been getting briefed into the council of elders by Mr. Lemayian.

"Are you bummed that I won't get to have a normal childhood?" Mwikali had asked, as her mom marveled at the red streaks in her hair.

"You're being your true self," she had answered, cupping Mwikali's face in her hands. "You're surrounded by friends who love you for who you are. That makes me happier than anything else ever could."

Her dad had stepped in beside them. "I'm so happy you're safe, Mwikali. You're really brave."

"Thanks. We all are," she had replied, glancing over her shoulder at her friends. After a few awkward seconds where she and her dad had just stared at each other, she had turned to Mr Lemayian. "So, what happened with the Red Oloibon? What did you guys do to him? Is he... dead?"

Mr Lemayian had called everyone's attention before answering her question. "Using the power of the council, we were able to vanquish the Red Oloibon."

"Power of the council? Vanquish? Are you guys like witches, now?" Soni had asked, amused.

"Vanquish means he probably burst into flames or something," Xirsi had guessed.

"As Oloibon, I was able to initiate your parents as official elders today. The ceremony was quick but it did the job. Your parents received the ancestors' blessings so that whenever they come together as elders, they're able to summon the power of all the councils that have gone before them. They have the power to vanquish, banish, or otherwise punish evil beings."

"So you probably formed a circle around the Red

Oloibon and then... Flames or no flames?" Odwar
had pressed.

"Flames," Mr. Lemayian had confirmed, before
continuing on quickly. "But what matters now is that
he'll never be a threat again. And that the four of you
succeeded in destroying the Forbidden Mask once and
for all. The world owes you its thanks. Asante."

He had turned to Mwikali and smiled at her hair. "In
the olden days, only warriors were allowed to dye their
hair red. It looks like the spirits you set free left you a
parting gift — a way for everyone to know what they
think of you."

He had reached into the messenger bag strapped
across his chest and — to her absolute delight — pulled
out her sketchbook. "Thought you might want this back.
We found it among Babu's things."

After that, their parents had insisted they all go out
to dinner to celebrate. Soni had pulled Mwikali into the
ladies' room at Tanu's Restaurant as soon as they had
gotten there.

"I'm starving!" Soni said, tucking a stray braid back
into her space bun.

Mwikali gave her reflection one last smile. "Me too.
Let's go."

Odwar and Xirsi were waiting for them right outside.

"Took you long enough," Xirsi grumbled. "Come, we've got our own table, away from the adults."

As she walked alongside her friends, she felt a tap on her shoulder. It was her dad.

Mwikali nudged her friends. "Go on, I'll be right there."

"I know you probably have a lot of questions and probably don't think too much of me right now," he said, wringing his hands together like she did when she was nervous. "But I just need you to know that I left because I thought it would protect you from all of this. It's not an excuse. I see now that it was the wrong thing to do, but it's the truth.

"When you were a baby and we took you to see my mom and grandma, they told me what you were. They could sense that you were different. I didn't want that for you. I wanted you to have a normal life. So, I thought that if I got as far away from you as possible, you would never find out about being an Intasimi. That your powers would fade away, and you would be safe."

Mwikali swallowed the lump in her throat. "My susus... I never got to meet them. You took that away from me, and so much more."

"I know. I'm sorry. I'll have to live with what I've done to you for the rest of my life. They loved you, and I know they're watching you right now, and are so, so proud of you."

He ran the back of his hand against his cheek, wiping a stream of tears away. "Anyway, there's a lot more I could say, but you should go and be with your friends. Your mom has invited me over for Friesday dinner next week. I hope that's okay?"

Mwikali nodded, and then before she could help herself, jumped forward and wrapped her hands around him. For more than a few seconds, they held each other tight, sobbing and squeezing twelve years of "I love you" into one single hug. Until Mr. Lemayian cleared his throat from behind them.

"Can I speak to you, Mwikali? With the others?" he asked.

After a few sniffles, they let go with a promise to talk more later, and Mwikali joined her friends at their table.

"I told you that I wouldn't hide anything from you, so I wanted to warn you about something," Mr. Lemayian said, looking around the table. "After today, all the creatures of the underworld will know about you. The Red Oloibon may be gone, but his army is still out there, regrouping and plotting their next attack. This is far from over. In fact, I fear it's only the beginning. You kids need to be ready. Because next time, they'll come at you with everything they've got."

They remained silent, taking in the full weight of his words.

"Mr. Lemayian," Odwar started, after a few seconds had passed, "you said that Mwikali's horn sort of levels up her power, right?"

"Yes, it's her Entasim. Every bloodline has one."

Odwar's eyes twinkled. "So, if each of us had our family's Entasim, we could get a power boost and be stronger for the next attack?"

Mr. Lemayian thought for a moment before answering. "Yes, but you would need to find them first. These things are thousands of years old. They were created by the ancient ones, the first ones. And it would be far too dangerous to go searching — you never know who has them or what they would do to keep them."

"Got it, thanks," Odwar said, quickly. "I was just curious."

They remained quiet as Mr. Lemayian walked back to the parents' table, but as soon as he was out of earshot, the three of them whirled around to face Odwar.

Mwikali grinned as she looked at him, already sensing what he was thinking, knowing that as friends — as warriors — they would stand by him no matter what.

"Spill it," Xirsi said. "I know you're not just curious."

Soni nodded. "Yeah, I know that look. Wassup?"

A mischievous smile crept across Odwar's face.

He leaned in so that only the four of them could hear his next few words.

"How would you guys like to go on an adventure?"

The End

ACKNOWLEDGEMENTS

Thank you first and foremost to my agent Lisa
Edwards for taking a chance on this lil' Kenyan girl.
You championed this story, answered my one million
questions with unending patience, and gently guided
me through this strange, new journey. I wouldn't be here
without you!

To my editors Christofere Fila and Oluwaseun
Matiluko, thank you for polishing this diamond in the
rough. You drew out the best in me and made this book
shine. It wouldn't be half as good without you.

To Melissa McIndoe, my awesome illustrator, thank
you for bringing my characters to life so brilliantly!

A special thanks to Alice Curry and her team at
Lantana Publishing for changing the game by seeking
out inclusive stories from around the world. All children
should be able to see themselves in the books they read.

To my children Ella, Lamu, and Tawi, you are the
greatest gifts that God has ever given me. Thank you for
the inspiration! I promise to always write books that you
can see yourselves in.

To my friend Julie, my ride or die. Girl, you have
been my rock through all the ups and downs. Thank you
for screaming when I landed a publisher, crying when I

finished my first draft and for the daily 29 minute-long voice notes that kept me going. Your friendship means the world to me.

To my parents, brother, and sisters. Thank you for your continued love and support, even from afar.

Eternal thanks to God through whom I live and breathe, and to the tens of thousands of ancestors who stand with me, beside me. Always.

About the author

Shiko Nguru was born and raised in Nairobi, the bustling capital city of Kenya. After a childhood spent climbing trees to find perfect perches to read books in, she spent her formative years in the United States, where she discovered just how cold a Midwestern winter could be and how much one person could miss the smell of freshly fried mandazis.

By the time she returned to Kenya, Shiko was sure of two things: that she was ready to spend the rest of her life in her homeland, and that she wanted to dedicate that life to telling her people's stories. The idea for the Intasimi Warriors series was born out of her love of African mythology, and the realization that precious few books featured characters that looked like her or her children.

Intasimi means "magical charm" in the Maa language of the Maasai people, and captures perfectly how enchanting she believes the people of East Africa's stories to be. She delights in bringing African history to life and looks forward to telling more stories filled with fun, magic, and adventure...

About the cover artist

Melissa McIndoe is an artist currently based in upstate New York. Her professional work includes children's book illustrations for small publishing houses and independent creators. She has also made storyboards for animation. In her free time, Melissa enjoys spending time with her dog, hiking mountains, and drawing comics. Oh, and tea. Lots of tea.